Book Two Of The Void Wielder Trilogy:

Legacy Of

Chaos

Cesar Gonzalez

This book is dedicated to my beautiful nieces:

Giavanni, Jacqueline, Madeline, and Ariany.

Legacy Of Chaos

Copyright 2014 by Cesar Gonzalez

Cover Art- Dennis Frohlich

Editors- Laura Hutfilz and Tony Held

Feel free to check out the Element Wielder website. There you'll be able to find character pictures, lore about the elements, and more.

http://cesarbak99.wix.com/element-wielder

PREFACE

On Planet Va'siel, there are a few beings that are born with the ability to wield certain elements. These gifted individuals are known as Element Wielders.

There are six basic elements and six advanced elements. Holding control of the advanced elements requires much more energy than a basic element. As such, wielders of advanced elements have become a rarity in Va'siel.

Basic Elements

Water: Water wielders control the element of water. Some advanced water wielders have been known to solidify water into ice.

Fire: Wielders who harness the very power of flames. The second stage of fire is blue fire. The third stage, which very few wielders have reached, is black fire.

Like water wielders, fire wielders are highly sought out for long missions. Their ability to create campfires in almost any environment has proven invaluable.

Void: Void wielders can wield all six basic elements; however, this power comes with limitations. Void wielders can only wield weak attacks.

No void wielder can wield blue or black fire, as those are advanced levels of fire. The only exception is Falcon Hyatt. For reasons unknown to him, he can wield basic elements and advanced elements.

Mind: Mind wielders can mold the minds of others. The extent of the control they have over people depends on the power of the mind wielder and the victim.

Some have been known to drive their enemies mad with false images of pain and suffering.

Mind wielders can also use their abilities to re-awaken thoughts that have been long forgotten. Most mind wielders are highly intellectual individuals.

Wind: Wind wielders can harness the power of wind, using that power in both defensive and offensive attacks.

Even though wind is a basic element, not many wind wielders can be found in Va'siel. The reason for this is unknown.

EARTH: These warriors are numerous in Va'siel. Their attacks are sturdy and strong. Their defensive abilities are some of the strongest a wielder can ever hope to create.

But their abilities go beyond the battlefield. Some earth wielders are able to mold and enrich soil with nutrients to create rich farmlands. The crops grown from capable earth wielders are some of the most delicious found in Va'siel.

The legendary warrior, Golden Wielder, was himself an earth wielder.

Advanced Elements

Space: The power of the cosmos is a mere plaything to space wielders. Not only can they summon the force of space to use against their enemies, but they can call forth universal anomalies like meteors, comets, and black holes.

Since there are so many mysteries in the great unknown that is the universe, the true extent to which gifted wielders can push their powers remains an enigma.

Poison: Poison wielders tend to be sick beings, both physically and mentally.

They possess the ability to create many attacks using venom and a variety of toxins.

In past times, poison wielders have proven useful during sieges, where they poison entire cities water or food supplies.

Darkness: Only the most cold-hearted and wicked beings can properly wield the powers of darkness. Wherever they go, pain and misery follows.

Dark wielders can control many of the forbidden wielding abilities that were banned long ago for their inhumane and unnatural power.

Chaos: Along with holy, chaos is the rarest of all the elements. In fact, in the past 10,000 years, Shal-Volcseck is the only known chaos wielder.

What exactly can a chaos wielder do? No one who has seen their power has been left alive to tell the tale.

Lightning: These wielders can summon the power of lightning. Most who practice this kind of wielding tend to be driven by offense. During battle, they rarely use their power for defense.

There are stories of exceptional wielders who have wielded red and green lightning, though most believe this to be just tales of legend.

Holy: Only the most pure and humble of beings can hope to control this power. As such, holy wielders are extremely rare. With each passing year, Va'siel has become more sinister and wicked, full of murder, deceit, and lies. It is for this reason that many believe that the power of holy will never return to such a cruel world. However, there are stories that indeed a holy wielder has been born in the small farming village of Asturia.

CHAPTER 1

"Hand over all your gold and nobody gets hurt," sneered the largest of the three bandits. He wore a red armor suit that encased his entire body.

"Yes, and don't even try anything funny. No one can get anything past the Volandis brothers!" shouted the smallest bandit.

Falcon sighed as he picked at the food. He hated when the fruit got stuck between his teeth. Where was he supposed to find a wood pick in the middle of the forest?

"Hey," sneered the large bandit. "Don't ignore us. Don't you realize that you're in the brink of certain death?"

"Yes," said Falcon as he took out a piece of the orange.

"Hey!" echoed the deep voice.

Falcon turned toward the men with droopy eyes. When he first heard the loud steps approaching, he had hoped it was Faith and Aya returning with food. They'd been gone nearly three hours. But to his sour disappointment, it was only these three men. "My companions were to wake me up when they returned. And, seeing as you're not them, you bumbling idiots have no business interrupting my little nap, do you?"

"Idiots, you say?" The medium-sized bandit laughed. "We already found your companions and slit their throats. It wasn't hard—"

"Funny, I don't recall having my throat slit," said Aya. The dark-haired girl was dressed in her usual white blouse and short black skirt. In her hands she carried what appeared to be a bag of stewed lamb. "I think I would have remembered someone doing that. How about you?"

Faith smiled. "No, I don't recall any attacks." Even from afar Falcon could make out her light-green eyes.

"Shut up!" snapped the bandit leader. "We'll teach you to mock the might of the Volandis brothers, and we'll start with you two pretty little lassies." The bandits sprang toward the girls.

Confident that they weren't in any danger, Falcon put his hand behind his head and lay back on the tree.

Aya was one of the best martial artists Falcon had ever seen. With her fists or baton she could hold her own against the strongest of foes. And if her martial arts failed her, she could always call on her element, water.

Then there was Faith, the only holy wielder on planet Va'siel.

The bandits dove forward with their swords raised above their heads. A second later they fell flat to the ground. The smallest one spat out the lump of dirt that had found its way into his mouth.

"What is this?" asked the bandit leader. He held his hand, touching the rainbow-colored shield they had run into.

"It's a shield," said Faith. "Had you paid more attention instead of rushing in mindlessly, you would have noticed when I put it up."

"No shield of fire, errr…I mean water. Or is it mind? Arghhh… whatever it is, it will not stop the Volandis brothers."

"Then maybe this will," said Aya. The blue emblem at the dorsal part of her glove shone brightly as water gathered behind her. The gust of water smashed into the bandits. They crashed into a tree. Dozens of leaves rained down over their heads.

"Damn wielders always ruining our fun!" exclaimed one of the bandits. "If I could wield the elements, I would put these teenagers in their place." The bandits hastily took off down the dirt path.

Falcon extended his arms. A water lasso shot out and wrapped around the bandit's feet and pulled them back. His emblem turned from blue to a light green as he switched to wind wielding. A burst of wind raised the brothers up to their feet.

The large bandit gritted his teeth. "At least I have the satisfaction of knowing you're just a void wielder and can only do weak attacks."

With a simple wave of Falcon's hand, a bolt of lightning descended from the sky, missing the brothers by a hair.

"B...but you're a void wielder," stuttered the bandit, his eyes wide. "I saw your emblem before you wielded. It was gray! How did you wield lightning?"

Falcon grinned. He had been getting reactions like this all his life. Regular void wielders could only perform weak attacks using the six basic elements. Falcon, however, was also able to wield advanced elements. It was both a gift and a curse.

"Did you really think we were going to let you free?" said Aya.

"The roads will be safer without you lot stealing from innocent people," added Falcon.

"What's it to you, stranger? What do you care what happens?"

"I'm a Rohad mercenary from Ladria. I don't like bullies who cause suffering for those weaker than themselves."

"What do you know about pain, you pampered brat? You don't even know the meaning of the word, not like us."

Falcon couldn't help but smirk at the remarks. Even at the age of eighteen, he knew more pain than most had experienced in their lifetime. The monster, Shal-Volcseck, killed his parents. He and his brother, Albert, had survived the attack and moved to the capital city of Ladria to begin anew. For years they lived happily, but then one night his brother disappeared after being accused of murdering the Ladria council. After that day the entire city turned against him.

"You're wrong, bandit. I know about suffering, but I choose to not impart the same fate that I've suffered onto others."

"I don't need a sermon from you. You defeated us already. Just get it over with."

"Get it over with? I'm not going to kill you, if that's what you're suggesting."

The bandit raised an eyebrow. "Then what? Torture?"

"You have a lively imagination, don't you?" Falcon pulled out a long piece of rope from his duffel bag and tied the three bandits to a tree trunk with it. "Don't worry, fellas. We'll tell the guards of the nearby village where to find you. You'll be sleeping soundly in your very own jail cell tonight."

The bandit mumbled something back at him, but Falcon couldn't understand him. After all, it's hard to understand someone gagged at the mouth.

~~~

They slowly moved down the narrow path that weaved through the forest.

"I still can't believe K'ran is your master," Faith said. "My dad fought alongside him during the Emblem War."

"K'ran is one of my masters, but I've been lucky to study with many great wielders," said Falcon as he stuffed a mouthful of stripped lamb into his mouth. "I studied with my brother, Albert. I also studied with K'ran and many Rohad professors. Some people think that all of the great professors

15

are at the royal academy, but Rohad has some wonderful teachers as well."

"You forgot Professor Kraimaster," said Aya.

Falcon frowned. "Oh yes. Him."

"What's wrong with him?" asked Faith.

"Nothing," Falcon mumbled. He didn't much feel like talking about the teacher who had made it his goal to insult and embarrass Falcon every chance he got.

Faith seemed to understand, because she then turned her attention to Aya. "What about you? I know you studied at Rohad like Falcon, but who did you study with before that?"

"My parents hired many private tutors. Even during my years at Rohad, they would still bring in tutors during the summer when I was off from class."

Faith nodded her head. "Wow, that's impressive. No wonder you're such a great water wielder."

"Thanks, but what I did is not that impressive. I had water wielders to show me the basics. You're the one who had to learn how to holy wield by yourself. I can't even fathom how it feels to be the only wielder of your class in the world."

"It does feel lonely sometimes."

For a minute the three of them remained quiet as they made their way down the leaf-covered path. A family of owls hooted from atop a branch. To Falcon, the sound was a sign that darkness would soon be upon them.

"I know that tree," he said, pointing at an old black Greir tree. "We're almost to my home. K'ran is going to be so shocked when he sees me." Aya and Faith followed close behind as he left the path and moved into the forest.

"It seems like we're going in circles," said Aya. "I've seen that tree before."

"Oh, no," said Falcon. "Many of the trees here look the same, but they're not. Don't worry. I spent a lot of time here. I know where I'm going."

"Of course," said Aya, her voice doubtful.

"That's so nice," Faith said. "You left the forests of Asturia and ended up with another forest as your backyard."

Falcon stopped as visions of Asturia rushed back. Memories of running through the garden with his mother. Memories of playing with Faith and Albert as children.

"Falcon." Faith shook him. "Hey, Falcon, are you felling well?"

He shook himself back to the real world. "Yes, of course. Let's keep moving."

After a few minutes of silence they came upon a small wooden cabin perched atop a hill. A small fence separated it from the hundreds of trees that surrounded it. Black smoke rose from the chimney.

Falcon walked up to the oak door and knocked.

"Maybe he's not home," said Aya.

"I barely knocked once. I'm sure he's on his way."

Falcon narrowed his eyes. He'd known Aya most of her life, and she wasn't one to get nervous. So why was she so jittery all of a sudden?

"What's wrong?" he asked.

"It's just that he's the closest thing you have to a father. What if he doesn't like me?"

"He met you once, remember?"

"That was only for a few seconds."

"I'm sure you'll be just fine." Falcon knocked again.

There was loud ruckus as someone struggled with the lock on the other side. A second later, the door creaked open, and there stood K'ran. His body looked as strong and muscular as the last time Falcon had seen him. His one good eye, though, appeared tired. The other, white, marbled eye remained as hard to read as ever.

Falcon gave his master a slight bow. "It is good to see you again. How are you, Master?"

"I've been better," said K'ran as he returned the respectful bow.

"You don't look so well, Master."

K'ran ran his hand trough the thick scar that ran down his left eye. "I'm afraid I'm suffering from a mild case of dysentery infection. Nothing major. My entire body is aching, but I'll be good after a few days of rest." He turned his attention to the girls. "Where are your manners? Aren't you going to introduce me to your friends?"

18

A pang of guilt hit Falcon. How could he have been so rude? "As you already know, this is Aya Nakatomi, my friend from Rohad Academy."

"Nice to see you again, sir," said Aya. She took K'ran's hand and shook it vigorously.

"It's good to see you again too." K'ran returned the shake.

Falcon motioned toward his other friend. "This is Faith Hemstath. She's the daughter of the mayor of Asturia, and she's also a holy wielder."

"Nice to finally meet you, sir. My father has many times told stories of your bravery." Faith stepped forward and embraced K'ran in a hug.

Falcon braced himself, not sure how his master would take the unexpected show of affection. But he was soon relieved to see that despite his initial shock, K'ran was smiling.

K'ran stepped back. He took ahold of her hand and stared at her white emblem. "Many believed that another holy wielder would never be born in such a wicked world. I'm glad to see that those rumors were wrong." K'ran let go of her hand. "Come in. I must hear everything that has transpired."

Falcon held the door open as the girls stepped into the cottage. As he walked in, he felt a set of eyes watching him. He turned and scanned the surroundings, but besides the leaves that danced in the wind, there was no movement. I must be going crazy. He closed the door and stepped into the warm cottage.

They sat on the old chairs that K'ran had built eons ago. He then served them each a mug of lime tea. A warm fire blazed in the fireplace.

"So how did you first mission go?" K'ran asked, taking a sip out of his mug. "I want to know everything."

Falcon ran his hand through his hair, not really sure where to begin. He decided to start from the beginning and go from there. He told him how his best friend, Lao, had turned on him and joined the Suteckh Empire. How the Ghost Knight had saved them from a Suteckh ambush. How the monster, Shal-Volcseck, had been hunting Faith for years, and he told him about the upcoming attack of the Suteckh on all the capital cities of Va'siel.

"This is dire news," said K'ran. "We must take swift action."

"Yes," said Falcon. "The Ghost Knight said the same thing. I'm going to gain an audience with the emperor and tell him what the Suteckh are plotting. I'm sure once he sees they're planning an invasion of every capital city of Va'siel, he'll mobilize his army."

"That's not what I'm referring to, Falcon. You have a much bigger problem here than the Suteckh. Why Volcseck seeks to acquire an emblem of each element remains a mystery, but we can rest assured that whatever his plans are, they're not good. From what you told me, I gather that Volcseck only needs a few more elemental emblems to complete his collection. A holy emblem is one of those emblems." K'ran stared at the golden-brown-haired girl with the sparkling white emblem on her glove. "He needs Faith's emblem. And to acquire it, he must kill her."

CHAPTER 2

"So what do you suppose we do, Master K'ran?" Falcon asked. "The last time I engaged Shal-Volcseck, he defeated me without lifting a finger, and he can sense Faith's holy energy; it's only a matter of time before he finds her."

"Tell me, Faith," asked K'ran. "How have you managed to hide from Volcseck all this time?"

"My father has managed to suppress my energy with his mind wielding, but my power has grown to the point where he can no longer suppress it. That is why I'm here. My father was hoping that a mind wielder of Grandmaster Zoen's caliber would be able to help."

K'ran bobbed his head. "A sound plan. Zoen is the strongest mind wielder I've ever known."

Faith and K'ran continued to speak as Aya played with the single leaf floating above her tea. She couldn't suppress a strange sensation that surged through her. She'd been so nervous about getting to know the man who had practically raised Falcon, and he'd barely acknowledged her presence. For a second she mused that perhaps it was jealousy she was feeling, but she shoved it aside. Faith had been a great friend, and she had never been the jealous type.

She yawned as she set the mug down.

"Are you tired?" K'ran asked.

"Yes. A little. Is there a place I can retire for the night?"

K'ran pointed toward a small hallway at the end of the cabin. "Go down the hallway and turn to the left. There's a room there I use for the rare times I get visitors. You and Faith can share it tonight."

"Thank you, sir." She excused herself from Faith and Falcon.

Like the rest of the cabin, the room was rather simple. Two small beds were placed at the end of each side. A small painting of the sea hung between the beds. By each of the beds stood an old looking cabinet with a wax-dripped candle on top.

Aya threw herself on one of the beds. The soft cushion beckoned her eyes shut. Before she even realized it, she was fast asleep.

Aya was vaguely aware she was in a dream. She saw herself ten years back, running through a field of long grass. Her younger sister followed behind her.

"I hide and you wait here. Got it?" Aya asked.

"No fair," whined her sister. "It's my seventh birthday. You have to be nice to me and let me hide first."

"All right, Selene. But I get to hide after you."

Selene waved her hand dismissively. "Yes, yes. Now count to ten, and no peeking."

Aya crouched and instantly lost herself in the long weeds. "One, two, three, four…." Even over her voice, she

23

could make out her sister's loud footsteps. "…nine, ten." She stood and glanced around. She was nowhere in sight.

She moved out of the grass fields and toward the pond. Her sister was so predictable. She always hid inside the old canoe.

"Found you," said Aya. But when she peered inside the canoe there was nothing. The baffled girl ran back into the grass searching for her sister. She spent then next ten minutes running up and down, looking for any sign of her.

"Fine," said Aya. "You got me. You can come out now." Silence.

"Selene! This isn't funny. Mom and Dad are expecting us back soon. Come out."

"Aya, he's got me!"

Aya's face turned pale as she ran toward the cry for help. She came out by the pond. Across it she saw a brown-and-red blur. In his hands he held her struggling sister. At least she thought it was her sister. It was hard to tell from the distance she was at.

"He's going to take me!"

Aya's eyes widened in recognition. There was no doubt. That was her sister. She untied the rope and jumped into the canoe. With shaky but determined hands, she water wielded it forward, but when she looked up there was nothing. No blur. No screams. No sister. Only a piercing silence.

"Selene! Where are you, Selene?"

"How could you allow this?" demanded a thick voice.

Aya turned. Her frowning father stared back at her.

"Dad. I...I don't know what happened."

Her mother materialized behind her father. She looked down at Aya, tears in her eyes. "How could you lose my little baby? You were the older sister. You were supposed to protect her, you wretched child."

"I'll find her. I'll find her."

Aya's eyes snapped open. "I'll find her!"

She pressed her trembling hand over her mouth. Did anyone hear me? A calming breath filled her chest when she noticed the bed beside her was empty. Faith had not gone to sleep yet.

She caressed her temples, trying to force the visions of her sister away. It didn't immediately work, but after a few minutes her breathing returned to normal.

Her nose wrinkled as the strong scent of smoke filled her nose. She turned to the candle, which had burnt down to its core. Only a pile of watered-down wax and dark smoke remained.

Aya picked herself up and grabbed the candle bowl, placing it gently by the window. Her heart skipped a beat as she made out the sound of footsteps on the roof. She broke into a smile. Only one person would be crazy enough to be on the roof in the middle of the night: Falcon. This was her chance to be with him alone for a while and catch up.

She quietly made her way out the window and onto the wet grass. Sparks of lightning flashed in the distance. A soft breeze moved through her black hair. The thought of going back for a blanket entered her mind, but she opted against it. She wasn't planning to be out for too long, after all.

"Hey, don't worry about the cold. Just get up here."

It was Falcon, and he was talking to her. How did he see me? She was certain she hadn't made a noise. But as she gazed up the roof, she saw that Falcon was talking to someone else; in fact, he hadn't even noticed she was there. Instead, he was sitting cross-legged on the roof. Besides him, Faith did the same.

"See?" said Falcon. "It's not too bad."

Aya felt a pit grow in her stomach. She quickly made her way back into the room. She couldn't believe she'd been so stupid. Of course Falcon was spending more time with Faith. He had a lot of catching up to do, after all.

Aya was twelve years old when she met Falcon on their first day at Rohad. The five years after that, they were inseparable. She didn't know what to make of her feelings for him, but she figured she had more than enough time to figure it out. After all, there weren't many other girls in Falcon's life. There was the flirtatious Hiromy, but Falcon never paid much attention to her. But everything changed once they'd gone to Asturia. There, Falcon reconciled with his long-lost friend, Faith.

Seeing Falcon and Faith together brought forth a symphony of mixed emotions. She didn't know what to make of them.

No. Those feelings are not important.

She closed her eyes and tried her best to push them away. But no matter how much she meditated, the river of emotions remained.

~~~

Faith remained quiet as she gazed at the stars.

"What is it?" asked Falcon.

"Um…nothing, I suppose. I thought I heard someone down there." Faith took a second look down at the grass below, but there was no one in sight. "I guess I'm just a little jumpy. That tends to happen when you have a psychotic chaos wielder on your trail."

Falcon remained quiet.

"Sorry," Faith mumbled. "We spoke more than enough about him tonight. No need for me to bring him up again." Faith wanted to kick herself for being so careless. Volcseck had killed Falcon's parents. How could she have been so tactless?

"Actually, that's what I wanted to talk to you about."

"Yes?"

"Back in Sandoria, when Volcseck showed up, I almost lost control…again. The element of chaos almost took hold of me until you arrived."

27

Faith thought back to that moment when Falcon's anger had overtaken him. He changed into some kind of monster.

Falcon continued. "The Ghost Knight suggested that when those feelings of chaos rage emerge, I concentrate my thoughts on someone I hold dear."

"Oh, and who is that?" She quickly wished she could take the question back. Of course Falcon would think of Aya. The bond between them was undeniable. To Faith's relief, Falcon didn't appear to have heard her, or maybe he acted like he didn't.

"When I was losing control and you hugged me, I felt a peace I have never felt before. I think it was your holy energy spilling into me. I've demonstrated that I can wield most of the elements, including chaos, so maybe my body is more prone to taking in your holy energy than most people."

"So you think we can use my holy energy to suppress the chaos energy inside you?"

Falcon ran his hand through his dark hair. "Maybe. It's certainly something to think about, don't you think?"

"Yes." She yawned. "But I think for now I should go to sleep. I'm tired, and I think better when I'm rested."

"Of course."

Falcon jumped down first. He landed on the grass without making a noise. Faith doubted she could be that graceful. A childhood of falling off roofs attested to that. Every time she found herself in high places, her heart rate quickened.

"It's really not that much of a jump," said Falcon, noticing the fear etched in her face. "What happened to that little girl that used to hop from tree to tree?"

"You forgot to mention that that little girl fell off more trees than she can count. I still have my share of scars to prove it."

"Here, I'll help you." Falcon jumped atop a log and grabbed Faith by the waist. He hoisted her down to the ground. Faith's leg tangled with his and they crashed to the ground. She fell safely on top of him.

"I'm so sorry," she whispered with hushed laughter. "I'm such a klutz. Are you alright?"

"My wounded pride notwithstanding, yes, I think I'm fine."

She became quiet as she took in his gaze and musky aroma. She stared at his eyelashes, realizing how the curl of them made his eyes stand out.

Falcon reached out and brushed back strands of her golden-brown hair.

Faith's entire world spun around her as she stood. She nervously patted off the dirt that had settled on her white-and-pink jumpsuit.

"Sorry," Falcon apologized. "I shouldn't have dropped you like that."

"No, no, no," said Faith, sensing the presence of death around her. It was the same feeling she always got when that monster came for her.

Falcon waved his hand in front of her. "What is it?"

Faith hastily searched the forest for any clue of where he could be. No matter how much she looked, she saw nothing. "I thought I sens—" A hand reached behind her and clenched her throat shut.

"Looking for me?" sneered Volcseck.

CHAPTER 3

Volcseck's tone was as relaxed as the last time Falcon had heard it.

"Let her go!" ordered Falcon as Faith struggled to break free from Volcseck's grip. The more she moved, the tighter he tightened his grip.

"I said let her go." His body energized. A second later a red lightning bolt slammed into Volcseck's chest. The attack dissolved harmlessly into him.

How did an advanced element not even faze him?

Volcseck tossed Faith to the ground and turned his attention to Falcon. "You again, boy. Didn't you learn your lesson from our last encounter?"

Falcon ran over to Faith, who was still coughing while clutching her neck. "Are you well?"

Faith bobbed her head. "Yes."

Satisfied, Falcon returned his gaze to Volcseck. He was garbed in a black cloak with red cracks. His face, as usual, remained obscured under the hood.

"Don't interfere with my plan, boy."

The low whisper sent a shiver down Falcon's spine. He ignored the feeling as he took out his katana. "Shut up. I won't let you touch her."

"As you wish."

Faith stood, putting herself between Falcon and Volcseck.

"What are you doing?" asked Falcon.

"What I should have done long ago. Giving myself up. No more people need to die on my account."

"I won't let you do that."

"We don't have a choice. He's too strong. Neither of us can hope to beat him."

Volcseck extended a welcoming hand. "Listen to her, boy. You don't have what it takes."

Falcon stomped his foot. How dare he? Who was he to judge him? And now he actually thought he was going to stand back and watch him take Faith? Never. He would do whatever it took to protect her. Even rely on that power. "You want more? I'll give you more."

"No, Falcon," cried Aya, as she rushed toward him. The ruckus had apparently woken her up. "You can't control it!"

Falcon ignored the pleas as he gave himself up to the chaos inside of him. His eyes burned with intensity. He looked down at his hands, which were now a dark brown with countless scars marred in them.

"I must say, boy. That is rather impressive," admitted Volcseck. "You seem to have access to all the elements. I believed I was the only chaos wielder to roam Va'siel in the last ten thousand years. Apparently I was mistaken."

"My name is not 'boy'! It's Falcon, and after today you'll never forget it!" His speech was more growl than voice. He pounced. Mere inches from his attack making contact, Volcseck disappeared in a puff of white smoke. A split second later he reappeared. This time he stood behind Falcon.

Falcon brought his hands together and formed a ball of purple energy. With a loud growl he released it.

Volcseck held up his hand. The attack changed course and returned to its sender.

"Frost wall," said Aya. A white ice shield materialized before Falcon.

Faith shot a beam of energy at the shield. A clear barrier reinforced the wall.

The ball slammed into the barrier. The ice crackled as the energy dug into the wall. Moments later, the attack dissolved.

"Good teamwork, girls." Volcseck nodded his head. "Halting a chaos attack is no easy feat, but it wont divert my plans. As for you." He pointed at Falcon. "Your ability to wield chaos could prove problematic for me in the future. I'll have to destroy you now." He wielded an energy ball, much like Falcon had done, except this one was triple the size. In the blink of an eye the ball blazed toward Falcon.

In his state, Falcon was barely aware of what was going on. But he knew enough to realize that a direct hit by the attack meant death. He tried to move, but his body remained frozen.

Seconds before the attack made contact, a blur hopped directly in its path.

There, holding the ball in his palms, stood K'ran. Green lightning surged through his hands, shielding him from directly touching the ball. He flattened his hands. There was a high wheezing sound as the ball disintegrated.

Volcseck put his hands together and bowed his head. "Master K'ran, it is an honor to meet such a legendary wielder."

"I wish I could say the same to you." K'ran let out a hoarse cough.

"Clearly, Master K'ran, you're in no condition for a confrontation. Step out of my way and go back into your home. If you do, you have my word that I won't bring an end to your legacy tonight."

The master took a long whiff. "I rather like the fresh air. I think I'll stay."

"So be it." Volcseck teleported to Faith and reached out for her. Red lightning surged around her. He drew his hand back at the last second.

K'ran clapped his hands. In an instant red lightning surrounded Aya and Falcon as well.

"I was going to take the girl and leave," said Volcseck. "But since you put a shield around her, I'll have to dissolve it by killing you first, Master K'ran."

Shal-Volcseck teleported behind K'ran and threw a punch. K'ran grabbed him by the arm and threw him over his shoulder. Before he slammed into the ground, he teleported again. This time he appeared in front of K'ran. He kicked high. K'ran crouched under the attack.

Falcon's features had returned to normal as he stood in his lightning prison, watching the duel. His two cellmates did the same.

Both masters were now fully engaged in a dance of life and death. A parry, an attack, a jab, a block; it was almost too fast to follow.

Falcon's mouth grew dry as he noticed K'ran's movements slowing. He knew his master well enough to know he shouldn't be tiring this fast. The illness was obviously taking a toll on him.

K'ran parried an attack. He dove in for a punch. But he suddenly stopped and stumbled back, going into a fit of sickening coughs.

I have to get out of here. I must aid my master.

"Your age betrays you, Master K'ran."

Despite his illness, K'ran smirked. "Oh, the irony. I'm not the one who is over ten thousand years old. Tell me, how have you stayed alive this long?"

Volcseck paused. "Those who give themselves to the chaos can attain anything." With a wave of his hand, a large cloud of raw energy appeared above them. The cloud dropped, threatening to crush them.

With one hand K'ran shot green lightning at the cloud. It held it in place, but Falcon knew that it wouldn't do so for long. His master was clearly overexerting himself.

Volcseck wielded a long lance in his hand. It appeared to be made of flesh, with veins and arteries pumping blood through it as if it were alive.

With lance in hand, he rushed toward K'ran. With his one free hand, the old master shot out the thickest bolt of red lightning Falcon had ever seen. Volcseck teleported. The bolt crashed into a nearby tree, which exploded into a thousand pieces.

Aya and Faith both gasped as the lance drove into the master's chest.

"No!" cried Falcon, standing in disbelief. He shook his head. This can't be happening.

The cloud of energy dissolved, and Master K'ran finally let his hands down. He staggered back and forth but did not go down.

"I've defeated entire armies, Master K'ran. What chance did you honestly think you had against me?" Volcseck drove the lance deeper into K'ran. There was a sickening sound of flesh tearing as the lance came out through K'ran's back.

Goosebumps rose on Falcon's skin as his master screamed in agony. He wished nothing more than to leap to his rescue, but the lightning wall encasing him prevented him from moving an inch.

"My intention was never to defeat you, Volcseck," wheezed K'ran. "I simply needed you close enough for this!" In a flash K'ran took Volcseck's hands and unleashed a storm of red lightning directly on them.

Volcseck laughed. "Pathetic. I have seen all forms of lightning. Even red is useless on me."

Blood poured from the master's mouth as he grinned. "All forms, you say? Let's test that theory." Suddenly the red lightning turned white. Falcon had to close his eyes and open them to make sure his eyes weren't playing tricks on him. He only knew of yellow, green, and red lightning. White was unheard of.

Volcseck grunted in pain. The lightning rippled and crackled through his hands as K'ran slowly drove him to the ground. The master was inches away from downing his opponent when a puff of white smoke burst from under him.

Volcseck reappeared atop the cabin. "Impressive, Master. I haven't witnessed white lightning since my encounter with the Golden Wielder. Tell me, how is it that you know that skill?"

"Don't fret about that. You should worry about what white lightning does to your body instead." Blood continued to gush from K'ran's mouth as he spoke. "It sucks your wielding energy. Essentially, it makes it impossible for a person to wield. Never again will your wielding cause harm to the people of Va'siel."

Volcseck chuckled calmly. "No, Master. You see? I didn't lie when I said that I am impervious to all lightning variants. You may have taken away some of my wielding abilities, but I'll get them back soon—very soon." His hands dangled by his side. "And when that happens, I'll be back for the holy wielder. Nothing and nobody will stop me."

K'ran coughed a stream of blood.

Volcseck bowed his head once more. "It was an honor to duel you in your last battle, Master K'ran." With those last words, he teleported out of view, the white smoke the only testament that he'd been there.

K'ran crashed to the ground. The lightning barriers he had created dissolved.

"Master…Master…." Falcon ran to K'ran. He threw himself next to him. "Master, don't leave me." He turned to Faith. "Do something with your holy wielding, please!"

Faith rushed by K'ran's side. She put her hands over him.

"No," said the old master, grabbing Faith's hands. "I am beyond saving, you know that."

38

Faith grimaced as her head hung low.

"What are you doing?" Falcon asked.

"I'm sorry, Falcon," she squeaked. "That was a chaos attack. The damage was too severe."

"It's fine, young lady," said K'ran. "I was dead the moment I used the white lightning. No amount of holy wielding would have changed that."

"I don't understand," whispered Falcon.

"Then don't try to. Just promise me that you won't forget who your friends are and why you fight."

"I won't, Master."

"It was my honor to have you as my student."

Falcon struggled to form words. His body ached, and his mind was a jumbled mess. "The honor was mine, Master."

K'ran grabbed both girls' hands. "Ladies, you two are the last good things Falcon has in this world. Watch over him, and guide him if he loses his way."

"We will, sir," said Faith.

"That's a promise," added Aya.

"Alexandra," whispered K'ran. "I can finally join you." With those last words, his eyes closed.

"No!" cried Falcon. He put his head over K'ran's chest, but silence had now replaced his once lively heartbeat. "Thanks." He knew K'ran could no longer hear him, but he had to say something…anything to put into words the gut-wrenching feeling he had lurking within him. "Thanks for putting up with me, thanks for taking me in, and thanks for being a father to me." Tears and rain had now turned K'ran's old tunic wet and cold, but Falcon didn't care. He simply kept his head on his chest as if somehow that would bring him back to life. What else could he do after losing a father for the second time in his life?

CHAPTER 4

The first rays of the sun made their presence known as Falcon set the last rock atop K'ran's grave. He knew of no better final resting place than behind the cabin. It was where he had lived his final years, after all.

"Do you want to say something, Falcon?" Faith asked.

Falcon looked up at her. "No, I said more than enough already. Let's just take a few minutes of silence to honor him."

"Whatever you want," said Aya. Both girls took a spot by Falcon's side, taking his hands in theirs. The three of them stood there holding hands and facing the ground.

"Perhaps I could say some words," came a soft voice.

Falcon turned. An old man with a large hump on his back stood in silence. His robe was pure black, a far cry from the usual bright-colored robes he wore. "Grandmaster Zoen, what are you doing here?"

"Did you already forget? K'ran was a good friend of mine."

"Yes, of course. How could I have forgotten?"

Zoen trudged in front of the grave. "I sensed Shal-Volcseck's presence and came as soon as I could. Unfortunately, I'm not as fast as I once was. I see that I'm too late."

Falcon nodded, aware that Zoen spoke the truth. The old grandmaster relied on a cane to walk, and even with it he moved at a snail's pace. He was old, very old. Falcon recalled his friend, Chonsey, once telling him that Grandmaster Zoen had been alive during the same time the Golden Wielder had been. If that were true, that would make Grandmaster Zoen over a hundred years old. He certainly looked like it.

With trembling hands Zoen set a jade-colored ring on top of the rock that adorned the grave. "Old friend, I now return to you that which you gave me long ago." A tear trickled to the ground. "I met K'ran a lifetime ago. He came to me a brash young man looking to make a name for himself." There was a serene sadness in the old man's words. "I still recall what he told me when he asked me to take him as a student. 'I will grow up to be one of the greatest wielders in Va'siel, you'll see.'"

This was news to Falcon. He had no idea that Grandmaster Zoen had once been K'ran's mentor, or that K'ran had been so brash in his younger days. The K'ran Falcon knew never cared for fame or wealth. He wondered what other things he didn't know about his old master.

"K'ran did become one the greatest wielders in Va'siel, but not only because of his physical strength," Grandmaster Zoen continued. "No, his greatest power derived from his gentle heart and his willingness to always put others before him. We shall always remember him like this." Grandmaster

42

Zoen's gaze met Falcon's. "I take comfort in the thought that his teachings and legacy will now live through you, Falcon. When in doubt, look back at his tutelage."

Falcon nodded, but inside he wondered if he could really be as kind as K'ran had been. Even now all he could think about was Volcseck and his many crimes: the murder of his mother and father, his many attacks on Asturia, his obsessive quest to kill Faith, and now the death of his master.

Yes, Volcseck was all Falcon could think of. And next time they met, he was determined to make him pay.

Once they had paid their respects, they took a seat on a set of tree stumps in the front yard. Falcon just couldn't bring himself to go inside the cabin. Too many memories dwelled inside those walls.

"Sir," said Faith. "You don't know me, but I'm here to see you."

"Me?" said the grandmaster.

"My name is Faith Hemstath."

"Hemstath. I know that name. You wouldn't happen to be Seth's and Nara's daughter?"

"Yes, that's me."

"How is your father? We have not spoken in many years."

"Thanks to the Rohads you sent..." She motioned toward Falcon and Aya. "My father's village and its people are safe. However, there is another urgent matter that he was hoping you could help with."

Zoen's features changed to those of curiosity. "Yes?"

"It's my element. Volcseck wishes to take my emblem to complete his collection."

Zoen rubbed his white, bushy goatee. "K'ran and I discussed this at length many times. Such a thing has never been done. I fear that doing so could bring forth catastrophic results."

"Like what?" asked Falcon slowly.

"I suspect that Volcseck will be able to create an attack that will end life in Va'siel as we know it."

The girls gasped.

"But why?" asked Falcon.

"I can't say. Only he holds the answer to that question."

Faith stood before Zoen. "Then I hope that you are the answer my dad wished for. My father can no longer suppress my powers, but perhaps you could."

"I can try, but holy is a strange element. It won't be as easy to block its energy." He extended his hand to her. "Come closer, please."

Faith took a few slow steps forward. She got on her knees and closed her eyes.

The grandmaster reached out with shaky hands. His right hand rested on Faith's forehead.

"What is he doing?" asked Falcon.

Aya lifted her shoulders. "Just watch. You'll see."

"Do re mi sa lu ke tore," chanted the grandmaster. A small ghostly creature forced itself out of Zoen's head. It had the head of a squirrel, but the body of a slug.

Falcon stumbled back, unable to believe his eyes. "What is that?"

"It's a mental memory," said Aya knowingly. "Seriously, Falcon, you should read more books."

"Books? I rarely waste time with those. They take away from my training."

"Books give knowledge." Aya pointed at the squirrel-like creature that had made its way down from the grandmaster's head. Since it had no legs, it slithered across his arm. "Those hide your energy. They come in very handy in stealth missions where the enemy has energy readers."

Falcon bobbed his head, finally understanding. "So they suck your energy."

"No. The ones that suck your energy are the memory leeches. You wouldn't want to use a leech on yourself because it would only drain you before a mission."

Maybe I should read more books. He gritted his teeth with anxiety as the ghostly creature struggled into Faith's head. It squealed loudly as it jerked its small body back and forth. A second later, it broke through. Its head was the first to disappear, and then its whole body was gone.

Zoen opened his eyes. "It is done."

"Is that it?" asked Falcon as the grandmaster removed his hand from Faith's forehead. "That was creepy enough, but is that all that it takes to keep Volcseck from sensing her?"

"Yes, that's it." The grandmaster gazed at the holy wielder. "Faith's abilities are exceptionally strong. It proved somewhat difficult, but her holy energy readings are now fully hidden."

Difficult? Falcon mused. He just placed his hand on her head for a few seconds. If that's difficult for him, what does he consider easy?

"Thanks, Grandmaster Zoen," said Faith. "I appreciate your kindness."

"There is no need for titles, dear. Falcon and Aya are Rohad mercenaries at the academy. They are obliged to refer to me formally. You, on the other hand, are not confined by those obligations. All my friends simply refer to me as Zoen."

Faith's cheeks turned a bright red. "Okay. Thank you, Zoen, sir."

Falcon and Aya eyed each other. In all their years at Rohad, they had never heard Zoen allow anyone to refer to him without his entire title.

"Don't thank me just yet, Faith. This energy blockade won't last forever. It will wear out in time."

"How much time?" asked Aya.

Grandmaster Zoen scratched his overly wrinkled cheeks. "That's difficult to assess. I've never dealt with holy energy before, and I can sense Faith's powers growing substantially." He pushed his cane hard on the ground as he struggled to his feet. "What I do know is that eventually even I will not be able to hide your energy."

Faith nodded slowly. "That is fine, Grandmast...I mean, Zoen."

Zoen turned his attention to Falcon and Aya. "Now to other matters. You were given a two-week mission to Asturia, but you stayed much longer than that. Professor Kraimaster informed me that he went to collect you and bring you back when the contract was over, but unlike Sheridan, you two refused to return."

Aya answered. "We had to stay behind. The Suteckh Empire was the one attacking Asturia, not bandits. We then discovered that they were plotting to conquer the capital city of Sandoria." She took a breath. "If Sandoria were to fall, that would put all the small villages between there and Ladria in danger, including Falcon's home village of Asturia."

"Falcon's home village?" asked Grandmaster Zoen, puzzled.

"Yes, sir. Falcon was born in Asturia but later moved to Ladria. The traumatizing events he suffered made him forget all about his time there, but with the help of Mayor Seth, Falcon regained most of his memories of his childhood."

"Hmmm, I see," said Zoen, rubbing his goatee as he usually did.

Falcon stood. "The Suteckh are planning an invasion on all the capital cities of Va'siel. If Sandoria had fallen, Ladria would have been next on their list. We couldn't let that happen. That's why we did not return with Professor Kraimaster. I know that my actions will have consequences, and I'm willing to face them. But please forgive Aya. I was in charge of the mission. I made the choice to stay, so I should be held responsible for—"

"No sir," interrupted Aya. "I stayed of my own accord. I should be held responsible as well. We are all responsible for own actions, right?"

Falcon shot a look of disapproval at Aya. Why did she always have to be like this? She drove him mad sometimes.

"While I admire your devotion to one another," said Zoen in a low voice, "There won't be any punishment for anyone today."

"What do you mean, sir?" asked a puzzled Falcon.

"Mister Calhoun told me what happened, and now so did you. I will speak to the Rohad council on your behalf."

Falcon was confused. "So if you knew what had happened, why were you interrogating us just now?"

"To see if Mr. Calhoun had been truthful. He seemed awfully sorry for leaving you two behind. In his despair he could easily have lied to me. I'm glad to see that that wasn't the case."

"Thank you," said Falcon and Aya in unison.

48

As the old grandmaster opened the wooden gate to head back to Ladria, he turned back to Falcon. "I suppose what Mr. Calhoun told me about Mister Keen is also correct?"

"Yes," answered Falcon with sadness in his voice. Lao had been like his brother for half of his life. They had done everything together, and now he was gone. "Lao was to infiltrate the Suteckh army and report back on their movements. But instead he joined them, and even led us into a trap. Many Asturian soldiers died because of his betrayal." Falcon calmed his shaky voice. "Afterwards he tried to kidnap the emperor of Sandoria. I defeated him, but I couldn't bring myself to kill him. I let him go. He was later found dead in a nearby cave. Someone murdered him."

Grandmaster Zoen sighed as he trudged back to Ladria. "That's unfortunate. He was a good young man."

Falcon's mind flashed back to the day he'd met Lao, to the many jokes they'd played on unsuspecting professors, to the many sparring sessions they'd had.

"Yes he was," whispered Falcon to himself. "Before he lost himself with the illusion of power, he truly was."

CHAPTER 5

It was midday when they reached Ladria.

Falcon stared at thick city gates. They looked indestructible, but he knew better. It would take more than thick metal walls to keep the Suteckh out of Ladria. Much more.

"Wow, the walls are as big as those from Sandoria," said Faith.

"Except the walls from Sandoria are made of rock, and these are made out of metal alloy," Aya pointed out. She turned to Falcon. "So, what's the plan?"

"We go back to the academy and await our next mission, but first we must warn Emperor Romus of the Suteckh Empire's threat."

"Sounds like a plan to me."

The three of them walked past the large gates and directly into the city's flea market. Stand after stand stood beside each other. The vendors waved their hands around and displayed their goods. Their shouts intermingled, creating a frenzied symphony of voices.

"Fish, get your fresh fish here!"

"Water, fresh spring water. Only two gold coins per mug!"

"Spring water is a thing of the past. Come and revel as you taste mineral-enhanced water from the east."

"Got an itch? Scratchy skin? Get rid of it with Xandi's lotions."

"Step forward and experience smooth silk dresses!" yelled a long man with an even longer thin mustache. A group of women in long dresses with fans in their hands stood before his stall. "They come all the way from Yangshao and need a home in your closet."

"Wielders, come get your emblems shined here. Don't be caught in a battle with a worn-out emblem. I personally guarantee you won't be sorry with the results. You three there," a vendor with a generous-sized belly said as he stood directly in their path. "I can see from the double dragon insignia in your collars that you are Rohads. You must also be wielders." He glanced at Aya. "Step over to my stall, young lady. I'll make that emblem look as good as new."

"Thank you, but I'm fine."

"Nonsense." The vendor looked down at the backside of Aya's glove, where all wielders carried their emblem. "Oh, a blue emblem, you must be a water wielder. But the color is so faded. Your poor emblem looks almost black, as if it belonged to a dark wielder. After I polish it, everyone will know that it's a water emblem. It will only take but a second."

"No, seriously, sir. I'm fine," Aya mumbled.

"Well," Falcon said, as they walked away a few steps, "he certainly gets points for trying. I don't think I've ever seen a vendor be so insistent."

"I'm still hungry," Falcon heard a voice whimper.

He looked back. A small girl had come out from behind the vendor's stall. She had dark eyes and wild, untamed hair. "Um, Papa. I'm still hungry. That piece of meat you got me was so small. Could I have some more?"

A look of shame registered on the vendor's red face. "It's been a slow day, honey. As soon as I make some money I'll get you some food." Disappointed, the little girl went back down to her spot behind the stall.

Aya turned and moved back toward the stall.

"What are you doing?" asked Falcon.

Aya set her right hand over the counter. "On second thought, my emblem could use a polish."

The man's eyes lit up. "You won't regret it." He took out a bottle of lotion in and poured it on the emblem. He then took out a cloth and wiped the emblem with it. "This is a lapis lazuli cloth. Many other cleaners use the much cheaper aqua cloths, but I only use the best for my customers."

"That's right," the girl added, pride in her voice. "My dad is the best in all of Ladria. No, in all of Va'siel."

Falcon stared in awe at the emblem. It shone brightly. The blue marble looked almost moving, like real water.

"How about you, young man? Your void emblem could use some polishing too."

Falcon stared at his grey emblem. The vendor was right. His emblem hadn't been polished in years.

"Of course he would like to get his emblem polished," answered Aya. "Isn't that right, Falcon?"

"Yes, of course." He set his hand on the stall and the man went to work. A minute later his emblem was as good as new.

Falcon was surprised to see Faith put her hand forward. Her emblem looked as if it had been barely been crafted. There wasn't a single speck of dust on it.

"A white emblem?" The vendor stared at Faith, mouth gaping.

The girl dashed forward. "Wow, a holy wielder. Papa, you said that holy wielders were extinct. Remember?"

"Did I hear you say holy wielder?" asked a man who passed by. He scampered toward them.

"Impossible!" cried a woman.

Soon there was a crowd around the stall, all straining to catch a glimpse of Faith.

"Don't disturb my customers," ordered the vendor. "Away with you lot, or I'll call the guards."

The crowd of people stepped back from Faith, though most of them still gazed at her from a distance.

Aya and Falcon eyed each other with interest.

53

"We should have perhaps kept the fact that she's a holy wielder hidden," said Aya.

"Yes," Falcon agreed. "We don't need the extra attention."

"Sorry about that," apologized the vendor. His mouth was still open more than normal. "I…I never thought this could be possible. For a holy wielder to be born in such a cruel world is impossible."

"Obviously not," said Falcon, growing a bit impatient.

The man shook his head. "Sorry. Lulu. Pass me my special bag."

Lulu crouched and disappeared under the stall. There was a loud series of crashing and slamming sounds. Moments later the girl came up with a dusty, brown bag. She carefully set it on the wood table.

"Special?" remarked Falcon. "It sure doesn't look like it."

"That's because it has never been used." The vendor reached inside and ever so carefully took out a yellow cloth. "My father passed this down to me. He spent his entire life hoping to use it. He died never fulfilling his wish."

With trembling fingers, he reached for Faith's hand. He set the wipe down on her emblem and began to wipe. "This is a celestial wipe. Legend has it that it's not even from this world. My father said that it came from another planet known as Elsire."

"Aha," mumbled Falcon in disbelief. "I'm sure it did."

Lulu's eyes glistened as she watched in awe. "Just you wait until Mom hears about this, Papa. She's going to go crazy. And you'll be the envy of every other polisher in Va'siel."

The vendor nodded as he wiped in a circular motion. He then took a step back. "Done."

"How much do we owe you?" Faith asked, admiring her pristine emblem.

"Nothing," said the vendor. "It was an honor to serve you."

"Nonsense." Faith placed ten gold coins in front of the man.

Aya reached into her pouch and set another ten. "And don't you dare give it back."

"I don't know what to say. Thank you."

They waved their goodbyes and continued down the road.

Falcon couldn't help but notice the small crowd that had gathered behind them. He felt out of place. Usually when people followed him, it was to whisper snide remarks behind his back. Even though it had been over five years ago, people had not forgotten the night his brother murdered the Ladrian council. But seeing Faith had apparently made the crowd forget all about him.

He ignored them as he continued down the lively road. Ladies-in-waiting marched behind noblewomen, white-clad priests chanted gospels as they moved through the crowd, ragged children scampered in between horses and through people's legs playing games of tag, and vendors and buyers haggled over prices.

Falcon cursed under his breath as someone stepped on his foot. That was the fifth time in the last minute. As he looked for the culprit, a man bumped him from behind. He gritted his teeth in anger. Fools.

Aya and Faith, on the other hand, didn't seem to mind the walk. They leisurely moved around people and waited for people to pass. After what seemed like an eternity, they reached the palace gates.

"May I help you?" asked the stoic guard. Behind him stood the grand palace of Ladria. Its walls were made of pure black marble. Dozens of cloth tapestries embroidered with the insignias of noble families hung from its walls.

"Yes," said Falcon. "We seek an audience with Emperor Romus."

"Do you have an appointment?"

"No we don't, but we were—"

"No one will be granted an audience with Emperor Romus without an appointment."

Falcon frowned. "Fine then. I would like to make an appointment."

"I'm afraid you can't do that."

"And why is that?"

"You have no family insignia on the back of your Rohad uniform. All Rohad mercenaries display their family crests with pride. The fact that you do not means you are Falcon Hyatt. Your brother is the traitor, Albert. Do you actually think our most serene Emperor Romus would agree to meet with you?"

Falcon clenched his teeth. "My brother is not a traitor."

"Oh, I'm sorry," apologized the guard in a sarcastic tone. "I suppose your brother wasn't the one who marched into the chambers of the Ladria council and murdered the council members in cold blood. He must have felt very brave, killing elderly men."

Falcon clenched his fist, ready to wipe the smug smile of the guard's face.

Aya stepped in front of Falcon. "Excuse me, sir. I'm Aya Na—"

The guard held his hand up. "I really don't care who you are. Anyone associated with this traitor is obviously a demented fool."

Aya took a breath. "Like I was saying, I'm Aya Nakatomi."

"Oh." The guard's smug grin disappeared, replaced by a look of nervousness. His eyes wandered to the pouncing lion insignia on her chest. "Oh, it is you, Miss Nakatomi. Please excuse me, I had no idea."

Aya waved her hand. "Forget about that. What do I have to do to see the emperor?"

"Any daughter of an esteemed council member can schedule an audience with the emperor."

"How long will it take?"

"If you sign up now, you can expect an audience in fifty, maybe forty, days' time."

Aya raised her eyebrow. "Forty days! Are you serious?"

"Forty days is more than generous, Miss Nakatomi. Why, if your parents weren't council members, your waiting time would be at least two hundred days."

"That's nice to know," said Falcon sarcastically. "C'mon, Aya. We're wasting our time here."

Defeated, the three of them scrambled away.

"I could ask my parents to speak to the emperor," offered Aya. "They can see him at a day's notice, but I doubt they will. They're already unpopular enough with the nobles because of the tax cuts they passed. Going up to the emperor with just our word and no hard proof will be foolish in their eyes."

"That's fine," said Falcon. "If you ask your father for this favor, he will totally lose it." He was well aware that Aya's father did not approve of her friendship with him.

"Don't say that. My father can be difficult and stubborn at times, but he likes you."

"It didn't seem that way when he kicked me out of the party your family threw," said Falcon, shooting Aya a look of disbelief.

Aya's face turned red. "Like I said, my father can be stubborn, but he also respects people who fight to change their destiny like he did. In fact, last time we spoke he actually sounded somewhat impressed that you managed to graduate from Rohad."

"That's nice," said Falcon, his voice dripped with mock amusement. "Instead of being a total idiot in his eyes, I'm only a minor idiot. Good to know. All you nobles are the same, always looking down on us."

Aya stopped moving and stared back at him with a pained look in her eyes.

"I'm sorry, Aya. It's just that I've been through so much lately. I didn't mean what I said."

"That's all right. You have a right to be being angry with us. It was we nobles who shunned you and K'ran for years, right? And now he's dead. And then you try to see the emperor and you can't because you are not a noble. I get it, Falcon. You have every right to be angry."

"No Aya, that's not what I meant."

"It's fine, Falcon," she said thickly. "I know exactly what you meant." She turned and trudged toward her home, which was located in the richest part of the city. "I'm going to have a word with my father. I'll see you later."

59

"Would you like me to accompany you?" said Faith.

"Thank you, Faith. But I have to speak to my father alone."

Faith nodded. "Very well. I understand."

Still red-faced, Aya turned and disappeared into the crowd.

"Aya, don't go," Falcon pleaded desperately.

"She can't hear you," Faith said. "And even if she could, I don't think she would come back."

"Why am I so stupid?" cursed Falcon.

"Don't beat yourself up too much, Falcon. The chaos element inside of you drives you to say and do things that you wouldn't normally do, especially in difficult times. Aya knows that."

"You think so?"

"Yes." Faith put her face directly in front of his. "But you shouldn't speak to her like that again."

"Understood," said Falcon, taken aback by the finality in Faith's voice.

"Good."

"We should head to Rohad Academy," suggested Falcon, attempting to regain some composure. "I haven't made my official debrief."

"Do you think they'll be angry at you for disobeying orders?"

"I don't know," said Falcon, hoping they wouldn't suspend his Rohad status. "Let's find out."

CHAPTER 6

"Wow, it's beautiful!" Faith shrieked. "I never imagined that the Rohad castle would be so gorgeous."

"What exactly were you expecting?" asked Falcon. "Walls shrouded in darkness?"

Faith couldn't help but giggle. "Well, yes actually. I mean, you guys are mercenaries, after all. I expected stone statues of warriors, training fields, and fortress-like buildings to serve as the Rohad headquarters. But instead I find myself in a beautiful lush garden filled with flowers." Seeing them made her realize just how much she'd missed her flower room back in Asturia. She hoped her dad was taking good care of it while she was gone. "I especially like the vine plants that are crawling up the castle walls. It takes years for them to get that way. It's all quite exquisite."

"You know, if you want to, you can take a look around the garden. It has a lot of flowers and plants that are native to Ladria, so you probably have never seen them before." Falcon pointed at a wall of green at the far end of the garden. "You see those bushes over there?"

"Yes," said Faith, gaping at the green barrier. It was long and easily stood over fifteen feet.

"That's a garden maze. At the middle of it are honey flowers. They smell beautiful this time of the year. You should check it out. I would love to give you a tour myself, but I have to report to my superiors. It's very boring stuff."

"Meet back here before sundown?" Faith asked.

"Sounds like a plan." Falcon took off down the brick road.

"And if I'm not here, it is because I'm lost inside the maze!" shouted Faith. "You know that I'm such a klutz."

Falcon looked back at her dismissively. "Don't worry, I'll find you."

I can do this, Faith thought. She marched up to the maze entrance and moved in. Immediately she was presented with a choice. She could go down the long path to her right, or the even longer path to her left. After some inner deliberation, she went down the left path.

"Excuse me," said a couple that squeezed past her. They were going the opposite way of her, which meant they were headed out.

"Excuse me, is this the right way?" asked Faith quietly.

The couple continued to cuddle and kiss as if Faith had not spoken. They turned the corner and disappeared.

Guess not.

She continued down the twists and turns, hoping to see someone else. But the more she walked, the more her hopes dwindled. There didn't appear to be anybody else in the maze with her, and she didn't seem to be any closer to getting out.

What would Falcon think if she couldn't even make it out of a simple puzzle?

She came upon a fork in the path. She eyed her three options. The left and right paths were shining brightly, as the sun came down on the leaves. There were even a few purple flowers sneaking out of the bushes.

The center path, on the other hand, had uneven terrain. Sticks that resembled long, crooked fingers protruded from the brown leaves. Long vines covered the top of the path, preventing any kind of sunlight from illumining the path. The entire scene gave her a sense of dread.

"I certainly won't be going that way," she mumbled to herself. She instead turned to the left path and started her descent into it. As she walked, she hummed and touched the wet leaves. The water felt refreshing on her skin.

"That path is only going to take you in circles," said a thick voice from behind her.

She hopped, turned, and shrieked all at once. A man stared back at her. He looked to be about her age, though he was much bigger than her. He had bushy brown hair and thick lips.

"I'm so sorry," said the man. "I didn't mean to bloody scare you. I saw you heading the wrong way and thought I should say something."

Faith steadied her breath. She looked up at him from top to bottom. He wore a blue Rohad uniform. An insignia of a gold-colored emblem was etched in his chest.

"You're a Rohad, I see."

The man nodded his head proudly. "Yes, actually. I'm one of the best."

"I'm sure you are," said Faith, smiling. "So why did you say I wouldn't want to go this way?" She pointed at the path before her. "It looks so pretty."

"Don't believe what you see. They make it look that way so people get trapped in here." He pointed at the dark, center path. "That's the path you want to take."

Faith winced as she stared down the gloomy path. "Are you sure? It sure doesn't seem safe."

The Rohad motioned her to come toward her. "Of course I'm sure. I'm a descendant of the legendary Golden Wielder."

"I don't think being the descendant of Va'siel's savior qualifies you to navigate mazes."

"Bloody fickle," whispered the Rohad. "What I meant to say is that since the Golden Wielder is my ancestor, I was accepted into Rohad Academy when I was but a child. I know this maze inside and out."

"I suppose I'll have to concede to your expertise," said Faith. "After you."

The bulky Rohad went into the dark path, followed by Faith. Goosebumps covered her body as the crooked sticks grazed her skin. A spider suddenly crawled in front of her and she staggered back. She loved all animals, but spiders were some that she still had a hard time getting used to.

The Rohad reached for her hand, but then he seemed to think better of it and simply tapped her shoulder. "Don't be scared. I'll protect you."

"I'm quite capable," she said, collecting herself. "Dark places get me a bit jumpy, that's all."

The young man snickered as he kept on moving. They came to another fork. Without giving it any thought, the Rohad took the left path.

Faith's spirits lifted as the dead branches became fewer in number. Healthy green leaves took their place. A bright light shone at the end of the tunnel.

"See?" said the Rohad. "What did I tell you?"

Moments later, they emerged into a large garden square. Her mouth gaped open. There were dozens of stone benches and a sea of different-colored flowers. At the center of the garden stood a water fountain that spouted a geyser of water into the air. Hundreds of white honey flowers surrounded the water fountain. Throughout the garden, there were over a dozen squares of grass where people sat. Some were enjoying a picnic. Other people stared at the sky, while others entertained themselves with kicking sacks.

"Hey, babe," said a bald-headed student who stood directly in front of Faith. Behind him was a group of snickering students. "I'm Delita. You look a bit lost. Is there anything I can do to help such a fine woman?"

Faith stared at the large student for a few seconds before speaking. "I'm fine, thank you."

Delita licked his lips. "No, you're not. Come with me. I'll show you a side of Rohad you've never seen before."

"Hey, Delita! Leave the lady alone," commanded her guide. "She's made it clear she doesn't need your help."

Delita held up his hands defensively. "Fine, fine. I was just about to leave anyhow." He disappeared into the maze. His friends scampered behind him.

"Sorry about that," said her Rohad guide. "Not all Rohad students are like that, I promise."

"That's quite all right. Thank you for coming to my rescue."

"No problem." He bit his lip. "So I noticed you're not wearing a Rohad dragon insignia. Are you from around here?"

"Oh, no, I'm just visiting."

"Well, I hope you enjoy your visit. It was nice meeting you."

"Thank you for helping me," said Faith. She waved goodbye and began to explore the garden. She didn't know where to begin. There were so many strange plants and flowers she had never seen before. She crouched and brought her nose to a small purple flower. It was so small that it could fit in the nail of her pinky finger, but the scent that came out of it was mind-blowing.

For the next hour, she continued to excitedly move about the garden. She experienced strange new smells and exotic new flowers. As time passed, the crowd of people diminished. They left until only Faith and the bulky Rohad remained. He sat atop a marble bench, sighing and mumbling to himself.

"I'm sorry," said Faith. "I don't mean to pry, but are you well?"

The student looked up at her with sad eyes. "It's nothing big, it's just that Rohad Academy holds a dance every year. The dance is tonight and I haven't found a date." He stared down at the grass, gloomily. "Don't get me wrong, I really don't care too much about the dance, it's just that my poor grandma sewed a suit for me to wear. I know she would be heartbroken if I were to not use it."

"Oh," said Faith, not really knowing what else to say.

He suddenly looked up with a smile across his thick lips. "Say, are you going with anyone to the dance?"

"I don't think so. I came here with my friend, Falcon. He hasn't mentioned it to me."

"Falcon, I know him. He probably hasn't told you anything because he goes with Aya every year."

Faith felt a slight pang in her chest. "Oh, does he?"

"Yeah, they do everything together." The fuzzy-haired student stared at her intently. "So perhaps you would like to go with me to the dance?"

She thought about it for a while. With everything that had happened, she didn't feel much like dancing. The gloomy Rohad's expression, however, made her feel bad for him. "Sure. I don't see any harm in going to a dance."

He smiled widely. "Thank you. Thank you. My grandma will be so happy. I can't wait to tell her."

"I'm glad." Faith looked up at the sun. It was close to the center of the sky. "Sorry, but I have to go, I have to meet my friend."

"No problem. I'll see you tonight at the dance."

"Sure." Faith ran into the maze, but stopped and turned once she realized she hadn't even given him her name. The poor guy wouldn't even know who to look for come nightfall. "I'm sorry. I've neglected to give my name." She extended her hand. "I'm Faith Hemstath."

He took her hand with a mischievous grin. "I'm Laars. Laars Masters."

CHAPTER 7

Falcon walked through the all-too-familiar marbled walls of the Rohad academy. They felt more cold and unwelcoming than usual. Perhaps it had something to do with Lao and Aya not being with him. Or perhaps it had to do with the fact that Professor Kraimaster was headed straight toward him. Falcon moved behind a group of giggling girls, hoping the professor wouldn't see him.

"Hello, Mr. Hyatt."

Falcon cursed silently.

The professor gazed at him. "I take it you were not zuzpended." He flashed his bare teeth. "Pity the council takez Grandmazter Zoen'z word over mine."

"Sorry to disappoint," said Falcon, annoyed at the professor's way of talking. Kraimaster had a tendency to drag on every S, making him sound like a hissing snake.

"Don't be arrogant, Mr. Hyatt. You were fortunate that Grandmazter Zoen came to your aid thiz time, but he can only protect you for zo long. Zoon the Rohad council will realize juzt what a nuizance you are. I zhall rejoice when you pack your bagz."

The professor walked away. His usual stoic expression was plastered across his face.

Falcon looked after him, silently wondering what he'd done to Kraimaster to garner such hate from him.

"Hey, Hyatt," came a voice from behind. He didn't have to turn to see who it was. Sheridan was the only person he knew who called people by their last name. "I see Professor Kraimaster and you are still getting along famously."

"Yeah, we're the best of friends," said Falcon sarcastically. He eyed Sheridan. He had on his trademark black coat that reached to his knees. The tattoo over his right eye stood out from his pale skin. "Anyhow, what have you been up to?"

"Not much. Just hanging out here as I await my next mission. I think it might be in either Belwebb or Missea. I'm hoping it's Belwebb. I hear that capital city has the most beautiful women. Not that any of them have a chance. My heart belongs to Hiromy, after all."

Falcon laughed. "I don't think the emperor will be too happy with you dating his daughter."

"I don't care about her father," said Sheridan, shrugging his shoulders.

"Have you even talked to her? Back when we spoke in Asturia, you didn't know anything about her."

"Well, we did speak a bit between classes the other day. I told her the weather was nice and she said 'yeah'." Sheridan's eyes were dreamy as he spoke.

"That's not very much."

He held up his hands. "But don't you worry. I plan to ask her to the upcoming dance. Once she sees how well I dance, she won't be able to resist me."

Oh, yes, the dance. With all that had been going on, he had forgotten all about it.

Sheridan's expression suddenly turned rigid. "Listen, Hyatt. About what happened back in Asturia. I'm so sorry. I didn't mean to leave you. If I could take it back, I would."

"It's fine, Sheridan. Your family sacrificed a lot to put you through Rohad. When Professor Kraimaster ordered you to leave us, you had no choice but to follow orders."

"I still feel really guilty. Nakatomi stayed behind with you and I didn't. But don't worry. The next time, I got your back. That's a bona fide Calhoun promise."

Falcon grinned. "Sure thing, Sheridan."

"What do we have here?" said a sudden husky voice. Falcon's childhood enemy, Laars, stepped up to him. Behind Laars stood his usual gang of cronies: Delita, Putin, Drusilla, and Elvira. "The brother of the traitor is back."

"But where is your best friend, Lao?" asked Drusilla. The skinny girl flashed her yellow teeth as she grinned widely. She turned to her sister. "What do you think, Elvira?"

The neckless girl looked up at the roof as if lost in thought. "I think the rumors we heard were true. Lao betrayed his best friend, and now he's dead."

"What do you expect from a peasant?" added Delita, rubbing his bald head.

"Shut up!" said Falcon, anger in his voice.

Laars looked back at his gang as he cackled out loud. "See how angry he got? It must mean it's true." He turned back to Falcon. "I knew it was only a matter of time before you two turned traitors."

"I said shut up!" Falcon knew that people were watching now, but he didn't care. Lao might have betrayed him, but he refused to stand idly by as people spoke ill of him.

"Or what?" asked Laars thickly. "I'm the descendant of the legendary Golden Wielder. A nobody like you cannot hurt me."

Falcon gripped his fist. The gray emblem in his glove turned solid red.

Laars' emblem turned dark brown.

"Relax, guys," said Sheridan, stepping between. "We are all Rohads, remember? What kind of example will you be setting for the students who haven't graduated yet?"

"I don't care," said Falcon. "Get out of the way."

Sheridan gazed at Falcon. "Well, what about the fact that you two will be stripped of your Rohad status if you fight?"

Laars and Falcon stepped back from each other.

"If you have a score to settle, then I suggest a tiaozhan. Me and Falcon against you." He pointed at Laars. "And one of your buddies here."

Laars smirked as he turned his ape-face toward Falcon. "I'm up for a tiaozhan. Are you, traitor?"

Falcon nodded. Usually he would have never taken on such a challenge. But he couldn't simply walk away like this.

"Let's go," said Sheridan. They walked down the hallway and out to the garden. "Don't ever make me do that again, Hyatt."

"Do what?" asked Falcon, confused.

"Be the voice of reason. It doesn't fit me."

"Sure," said Falcon, though he wasn't paying much attention to Sheridan anymore. His concentration was on the tiaozhan. He'd never been good at it. The precision that was required in the game was not his strong suit. He found himself wishing Aya were with him. She could surely get them an easy win.

They moved past the maze and around the castle.

Elvira's knees knuckled loudly as they walked down the path toward the tiaozhan fields.

"You should have a doctor check that, Nord," said Sheridan. "Your bones snapping like that is not normal."

"Shut up," hissed Elvira. "Mother says that's what makes me special."

Sheridan laughed. "Whatever you say."

"Each team gets two shots," said Laars as they reached the wide-open range. "We'll go first."

74

"Fine," said Falcon. He looked up and noticed the sun had travelled two-thirds through the sky. He had to hurry. Faith could be already looking for him.

"Remember," said Sheridan. "This is a test of precision and teamwork, so none of that super-powerful wielding you're so fond of."

"Yes, I know," said Falcon, sounding much more confident than he felt.

Laars and Delita stepped behind the white line drawn on the grass. About one hundred meters ahead stood a large steel wall. It had five different animals depicted on it. Each animal held its mouth open. Inside each of their mouths was a hole of a different size. The biggest of the holes belonged to the ox. It was about the size of two human heads, which meant it was the easiest to get an attack through, but it also was only worth twenty points.

Falcon watched in silence as Laars and Delita held their hands up.

"Hiyaaah!" they yelled in unison.

Water left Delita's fist.

An earth spike flew out from Laars' hand.

Falcon cursed silently as the attacks met in mid-air and combined into a single ball. A second later, the ball travelled through the second-largest hole.

"That's forty points!" yelled Laars. His gang patted him on the back as they congratulated him.

Falcon and Sheridan hustled close together.

"So should we go for forty points too?" Sheridan asked.

Falcon concentrated, struggling to make a choice. They could go for the sixty-point hole, but that was the third-smallest one in the wall. He wasn't sure he had enough for such an attack. If it was just him, he could easily hit it. But to form a harmonious attack with another person required much more precision. After much deliberation he decided to take the easier route. "Let's just go for the forty points."

Sheridan gave him a thumbs-up.

They stood behind the line and held their hands up.

Falcon aimed his hand at the lion's mouth at the bottom right-hand corner. His emblem turned crimson as a line of fire flew forward.

He held his breath as his flames met Sheridan's moon rock. The attacks collided and formed a perfect sphere that whizzed through the lion's mouth.

"Eat that!" shouted Sheridan, pointing toward Laars' gang. "That's forty points."

Laars frowned. He leaned over to Delita and whispered something in his ear. Then they released their attack.

Falcon's jaw dropped as the their attack meshed together and travelled through the dragon's mouth.

"One hundred points!" cried Laars. "This game is as good as over."

Sheridan turned to Falcon; a frown had replaced his smile. "We have no choice but to go for the dragon and tie the match. Anything else will be useless."

Falcon eyed the petite hole in the dragon's mouth. His spirits dwindled down to the darkest corner within himself. "That thing is about three inches wide."

"I know. But we can do it." Sheridan patted Falcon's back. "Listen, that last attack was losing air halfway through the air. We need to shoot straight. Go with earth this time."

Falcon bit his lip. "Are you sure? I think we are better off going with water and shooting a little high. The attack will arc down and go in. Hopefully."

"Trust me. Straight and true."

Sheridan sounded so hopeful that Falcon was left with little choice but to nod in agreement. "Earth it is."

They stood behind the line.

"Traitor," called Laars from behind him. His gang snickered in suppressed laughter.

Falcon breathed in, trying to ignore the comment. But no matter how hard he tried, Laars' comment echoed in his head. He was so lost in his own thoughts that it barely registered when Sheridan let out his ball of stardust.

Panicking, he shot an earth rock forward. The large shapeless chunk of rock slammed into the stardust, dissolving into a puff of smoke. A second later the rock clanked loudly against the wall. Nowhere close to the circle where he had aimed.

Laars and his gang cheered loudly as they hopped and high-fived one another.

"See?" jeered Laars. "One hundred and forty to forty. It wasn't even close."

Falcon's air left him as he rubbed his aching head.

"Don't worry about it," said Sheridan. "We'll get him next time."

"There won't be a next time, losers," said Laars.

"Yes, losers," added Putin.

Unable to continue hearing their celebration, Falcon hastily made his way back to the castle. His insides fumed more with each step he took. How could he have allowed Laars to insult his friend and get away with it?

"Relax, Hyatt."

"I'm relaxed," said Falcon, feeling anything but relaxed. "Listen, I'm going to my room. Faith might be there looking for me."

"Are you sure you're well?"

"Yes. See you around." He marched into the castle and down the long corridors. As he passed the dining room, he noticed Aya sitting on a table, with a group of student girls gathered around her.

He collected his breathing and marched toward her.

"What about wielding water out of thin air?" said one of the girls. "I tried everything the books say, but I always fail."

"Me too," added a freckled-faced student. "It's impossible." The rest of the students nodded in agreement.

Aya set her spoon down. "It's not impossible. You simply have to—" Her eyes met Falcon's. "Listen, girls. Can we continue this conversation at another time?"

"Yes. Of course, Miss Nakatomi," said the freckled student. She and her group of starry-eyed friends thanked Aya and walked away. Falcon noticed a slight spring in their step.

"Well, I was right," said Aya. "Both my father and mother refuse to go see the emperor. They say there's not enough proof to back up our claims."

"It's fine, Aya. We expected as much, right?"

"Yeah, I suppose so."

Falcon gathered his strength. "Listen. About earlier—"

"Don't worry about it. I know the chaos element drives you to say things you don't really mean."

He took a seat beside her. "No, Aya. I can't blame chaos for my actions. Please accept my apology. I promise it won't happen again."

Aya smiled. "You know, all this sounds awfully familiar." She took a sip out of her clear bowl of broth. "You still owe me a favor for that, remember?"

"It's been five years, but I haven't forgotten."

"I forgive you, Falcon." She leaned in close. "Don't do it again."

He sighed with relief. "Thanks."

"Hello, Sheridan," said Aya, looking past Falcon.

"Hey, Nakatomi."

"I came to find you, Falcon."

"Me?" asked Falcon, confused. "Why? We were together barely a few minutes ago."

"Are you going to finish that?" asked Sheridan, pointing at Aya's bowl of broth.

"Go right ahead," said Aya.

Sheridan's body trembled as he took the broth and downed it in one gulp. He licked his lips.

"So, why were you looking for me?" asked Falcon impatiently.

Sheridan licked the broth that had spilled on his fingers. "Oh, yes. Don't go to our old dorm room we used to share on the student wing. We're full-fledged Rohads now. We have been assigned our very own mercenary rooms."

"That's fine, I suppose," said Falcon, failing to see Sheridan's enthusiasm.

Sheridan clutched his chest. "It's more than just fine. They have a cold box filled with any food you could think of. And if there's something missing, all you do is have Fletcher - that's the cook lady - bring it up to you. She doesn't like me much because I keep on putting in special orders at midnight. But I can't help it when I get hungry, can I?"

"You should learn to control your appetite," said Aya. "On missions you don't get prepared meals when it pleases you."

"Ahhh, Nakatomi. So professional, as always. You have to stuff your mouth with what you have while you can." He suddenly stopped talking and took off toward a student who was about to dump their tray of food in the trash bin. "Don't waste that!" He picked up an untouched grilled drumstick and stuffed it in his mouth.

"Should we pretend we don't know him?" Falcon asked. He jumped as Faith took a seat in front of him.

"There you are," said Faith. "I've been looking all over for you."

"I'm sorry, Faith," said Falcon. "I got sort of sidetracked."

She smiled. "No worries. Besides, I met some nice people."

"Nice people in Ladria?" said Falcon. "That doesn't sound like the Ladria I know."

"Perhaps not for you, Hyatt," said Sheridan. He took a seat beside Faith as he spat out a bare bone from his mouth. "You look like you climbed atop the biggest ugly tree in Va'siel and fell from it, and on the way down you hit every branch on the tree, quite hard I might add. But us good-looking folk have no problem making friends. I'm not saying is fair, but it is what it is."

"Real funny," said Aya. "Anyway, who did you meet, Faith?"

"Some guy inside the maze. He seemed really shy, but he was nice. He even asked me to the dance tonight."

"Really?" said Aya, sounding much more interested than Falcon expected of her.

"I didn't really want to go, but I felt bad for him. So I said yes."

Falcon felt a jumble of emotions coursing through him. He wasn't sure if he should be angry, happy, confused, or sad.

"Maybe you know him," said Faith. "His name is Laars Masters."

Everyone's mouths fell open.

"What?" asked Faith. "Did I say something wrong?"

CHAPTER 8

"So let me get this straight," said Falcon, as he walked into his new dorm. Faith, Aya, and Sheridan were with him. "Laars guided you through the maze and then came to rescue you from a guy called Delita?"

"Yes," said Faith. "Though I wouldn't really call it a rescue. Delita was simply a bit too friendly. Laars asked him to leave me alone."

Falcon frowned. "And after all this, he asked you to the dance?"

"Yes, that's correct."

Falcon took a seat on the large bed.

"What did I tell you, Hyatt?" said Sheridan. He opened the icebox that rested on a counter and took out a tray of milk cream. "I told you the dorms were spacious."

Being a full-fledged Rohad certainly came with its perks. There was an oversized bed, a bell to ring for food service, a chandelier with over a dozen candles, an icebox with plenty of food, silk curtains that adorned the two crystal windows, and an extensive library of books ranging from battle tactics to wielding history.

Falcon absentmindedly gazed around the room. It was rather impressive, and at any other time he might have been admiring his new accommodations. But at the moment he still couldn't wrap his head around what Faith had told him.

"It doesn't make any sense," said Aya. "Why would Laars invite Faith to a dance? What does he have to gain from it?"

"He must be up to something," said Falcon. "It's the only explanation."

"Why would he have to be up to something?" Faith asked as she admired a flower drawing that hung on the wall.

"Because that's who he is," said Sheridan. "He has always enjoyed tormenting Hyatt. I'm sure Masters knew that asking Hemstath to the dance would make Hyatt jealous."

From the reflection in the small mirror, Falcon saw his face turn beet red. "I'm not jealous. I'm simply aware of how cruel Laars can be. I don't want him to hurt Faith. It's better if she doesn't go with him."

"Isn't that her decision?" said Aya. "She is the one who got invited, after all."

"Excuse me?" asked Falcon. "You know how Laars can be."

"I know how he is. That still doesn't change the fact that this is Faith's decision to make."

Falcon's jaw dropped. How could she possibly entertain the idea of Faith going to the dance with that pompous brat?

"Aya's right," said Faith.

Falcon's jaw dropped even more.

Faith continued. "I don't know what sort of history you have with him, Falcon. But I gave my word that I would accompany him to the dance. I always keep my word."

Falcon clenched his teeth. He knew Aya was right. He had no right to tell Faith who she could or could not go to the dance with. Nonetheless, he couldn't help the uneasy feeling he got when he pictured Laars and Faith together at a dance.

That's it. The dance!

The idea came to him like a sudden ray of light. There was a way for him to get close to the emperor after all.

Falcon got up and rushed to the door. The dance was tonight. He had to hurry if he was going to make it on time.

"Where are you going?" called Aya after him.

"To meet an old friend," said Falcon, rushing out into the hallway.

He ran out the Rohad gates, through the buzzing flea market, past the pubs, and over the water bridges. He reached the city gates. The Rohad mission chart hung on the pie shop walls. He caught a whiff of baked apple as he read the names on the chart. Soon enough, he found the person he was looking for. According to the list, she was due to be back in less than an hour.

"How convenient," he whispered to himself as he took a seat on the stone bench.

Moments later he saw her. Her wavy, chestnut-colored hair danced up and down. She wore a tight-fitting blue polyester suit. Falcon had never seen her wearing anything that wasn't blue. He suspected it had something to do with her element.

She walked alongside two other girls. Her companions wore red Rohad uniforms, which meant they were fifth-year students.

"Hey," cried Hiromy as she laid eyes on him. She dropped a wheat roll she had been eating and ran toward him. Falcon was used to Hiromy's bursts of energy. But even he was caught off guard when she jumped on him and gave him a hug.

"Good to see you, too," said Falcon.

She took a step back. "Sorry." She ran her hands through her hair. "I shouldn't get too excited. Daddy would kill me if he saw me. I'm simply so glad to see you. I thought something had happened to you since you didn't return when you were scheduled to."

"I got a little preoccupied," said Falcon. "So, where are you coming from?"

"I just finished my first mission as a Rohad," said Hiromy with pride in her voice. "I had to retrieve a stolen artifact from Wadsworth Village." She motioned at her clothing. "This suit actually came in handy. It makes you quite nimble when you have to sneak past guards."

"Really?" said Falcon, surprised. "I didn't think your father would let you take on such a dangerous mission."

"He didn't. As far as he knows, I was out on a mission getting some diplomatic scrolls signed. Can you imagine me sitting at another one of those boring political dinners?" She stuck out her tongue in disgust. "Yuck."

Falcon had never given it much thought, but now that he focused on it, he supposed the life of the emperor's daughter could be hard, too. The fact that her father was extremely protective of her probably made everything much worse.

"So what are you doing here?" asked Hiromy. "Waiting for your friend, Aya?" She said Aya's name as if it was some type of deadly infection that should never be mentioned.

"I was actually waiting for you."

Her eyes lit up. "Me, really?"

"I don't know if you heard. Well of course you heard. It's happening in your home. I barely heard about it myself. It's no big deal. But maybe you could, or would want to…" He took a breath, surprised at how hard this was turning out to be. It was just a way to get close to the emperor, after all.

Hiromy smiled. "Relax, Falcon."

He gripped his shirt with a tight grip. It seemed to release some of the stress. "I'm sure it's a long shot. But would you consider going to the dance with me tonight?"

Hiromy looked back at her two friends, and back at Falcon. A wide grin spread across her face. "Yes! Of course."

"But I thought you said you didn't want to go," blurted out one of Hiromy's companions. "Something about your dad bugging you about attending events that you didn't want to go to."

Hiromy shot a look of disapproval at her outspoken friend, who quickly closed her lips.

"If you can't go, I understand," said Falcon.

"No. Miriem doesn't know what she's talking about. I want to go. I'll see you at my dad's palace tonight, yes?" Hiromy grabbed her friends by the hands and pulled them away. They were no doubt headed to the palace.

"Yes. See you there."

Once Hiromy had walked out of view, he pumped his fist. He'd done it. He had found a way to get close to the emperor.

~~~

Falcon walked into the dance with Aya on one hand and Faith on the other.

Aya wore a glimmering blue dress. Faith, on the other hand, had donned a pink-and-brown dress. A flower rested over her right ear.

Falcon wore a simple blue suit with a white shirt underneath.

A giant chandelier with hundreds of candles hung from the domed ceiling. On the left side of the room, the Ladria orchestra played soothing classical music.

"There's Laars over there," said Faith, pointing at the bushy-haired student standing by the food table. "I'll see you two later tonight."

Falcon tried to suppress the anger in his voice. "Just be careful, Faith."

Faith smiled. "Don't worry. I will."

"Stay focused," said Aya. "Remember what we're here for? We have to let Emperor Romus know what the Suteckh are plotting."

"We? You mean me. You won't make it anywhere close to the royal table, not without your parents."

"I know. But better to be here doing something than back at the dorms doing nothing. At least I'll get to dance with someone. You know how I love to dance."

"Oh, yes. I know." Throughout his years at Rohad, Falcon had attended more than one dance with Aya. The day after every dance, he would wake with blisters on his feet. They were some of the most painful memories he had at Rohad, but strangely some of the fondest as well.

"Good luck," said Aya. "Tell me how it goes."

"I will." Falcon scanned the large palace hall for Hiromy. She was going to be hard to find in such a packed room. There were long tables along the right side of the wall filled with food. Everything from local foods like Beruda steaks, grove juice, pichion meat, and dried berries to imported honey-dipped almonds, red bean buns, seaweed fish, and sweetened white meat.

A soft tap landed on his shoulder. He turned and found himself face-to-face with Hiromy. She wore a luxurious white-and-blue dress. Her hair was fixed in two hooped ponytails.

"You've been here long?" she asked.

"No, not really." He handed her a blue rose.

"Oh it's beautiful." She grabbed his hand. "Follow me. I want you to meet Dad."

Talking to the emperor might be easier than I thought.

But when Falcon got to the royal table, he quickly saw how wrong he was. Emperor Romus sat at the end of a long table. He was a short man with an untamed mustache. The table was filled with nobles, army commanders, and generals.

The emperor pulled out the empty chair on his right side. "Go ahead, my beautiful daughter."

"Thanks, Daddy," said Hiromy, taking a seat. She looked at Falcon. "You can sit in front of me."

Falcon looked at the chair Hiromy pointed at. How does she expect me to sit there? There was a nobleman sitting on it.

The man held his nose up to the air. Falcon didn't know who he was, but the fact that he sat on the emperor's left side was a clear testament to his royal status.

Falcon stood behind Hiromy. "There's someone there."

"It doesn't matter," responded Hiromy, matter-of-factly. "Nobleman Loss was just leaving."

Nobleman Loss's eyes darted about the table. "I assure you, young miss, that I had no intention of leaving."

Hiromy turned to the emperor. "Dad, wasn't Mr. Loss leaving?"

The entire table went quiet.

"Nobleman Loss," said Emperor Romus, pulling at his mustache. "Weren't you just saying you were about to step out for some fresh air?"

Nobleman Loss's shade of color changed a few pigments. "Oh, yes. I get an awful headache when I don't get some fresh air at nights. It would do me much good to step outside for a moment." He turned to Falcon. "Go ahead, you can sit here while I'm gone, Mister... I'm sorry, I didn't get your name."

"Falcon Hyatt."

A loud gasp made its way through the table. Obviously they hadn't expected to be spending the evening with him.

"What?" hissed Nobleman Loss. "I have to give up my chair to the brother of the traitor?"

"You have to give up your seat for my friend," said Hiromy, glaring at the nobleman.

The man raised his fist and opened his mouth. But then he brought it down and stomped away.

91

Falcon felt his face redden with heat. "Listen. I don't want to cause any trouble. I just wanted to speak to you, Emperor Romus."

The short emperor eyed him suspiciously. "Then why didn't you set up a meeting with me?"

"I'm afraid that would take too long. I need to speak to you now."

"That won't do. As you can see, I'm hosting a party at the moment."

"With all due respect, sir, this is not the time for parties. The Suteckh Empire is launching an attack on the capital cities of Va'siel. It's highly likely that Ladria will be next."

The emperor tossed a grape into his mouth. "Don't waste your breath. Word has reached me of the Suteckh attack on Sandoria. And I fail to see how a conflict between those two backward cities has anything to do with Ladria."

Falcon tried to keep his voice as respectful as possible. "It's not only Sandoria that was attacked. I'm sure you are aware that the Suteckh Empire sacked the Asian city of Zhangshao. They have set their eyes on conquering the entire planet."

An imposing man who wore a dark uniform with countless pins and ribbons on his chest stood. Falcon recognized him immediately. He was Chonsey's father, the general of Ladria's army. "Our army is more than a match for the Suteckh. Even if your story were true, we could take care of them with ease."

"But it's not only them," Falcon countered. "The Suteckh have garnered the support of many of the outskirt clans. Including the Northern Barbarians, the Omega warriors, the Hollow Clansmen of the Lost Sea, and the Scaiths—"

"Do you have proof of these wild claims?" the general asked.

"Yes, the Ghost Knight himself told me."

The table erupted in a fit of scornful laughter.

The general sighed heavily. "The Ghost Knight? That's your proof? This is ridiculous."

"Who is this Ghost Knight you speak of?" asked Emperor Romus.

The General's voice boomed. "He's a nobody who roams the land pretending to be a hero. His word is not to be trusted, sire."

"That's not true," snapped Falcon. "The Ghost Knight is simply trying to help everyone, including you."

"That's enough!" shouted Emperor Romus. "I had enough of this conversation. Remove yourself from my presence at once."

Falcon held up his finger. "But you must see the urgency of the matter."

The emperor slammed his fist on the table. "Enough, I say!"

"Fine. Stay blind." Falcon stood and stormed away. He should have expected as much from the leaders of Ladria. They had always been too prideful to listen to anyone but themselves.

As he headed toward the door, a bulky figure obstructed his path. "Going somewhere, traitor?"

"Get out of my way, Laars."

"Don't tell me you're still sore because of the beating me and Delita gave you."

Falcon pursed his lips. "I said get out of the way."

Laars licked his thick lips. "Nice little dame you brought back from Asturia." He looked over at Faith, who was sitting at a table speaking to the twin sisters, Drusilla and Elvira. "I would have taken my sweet time too if I had found a hot girl like that."

"You better not do anything to her."

Laars put up his hands innocently. "Relax. I'm simply getting her a drink." He held up a cup of red juice. "Of course I might accidentally spill it on her dress. Then being the gentleman that I am, I will have to escort her to my room so she can change into something more comfortable."

Falcon had heard enough. He clenched his fist and grabbed Laars by his collar. "I'll teach you to—"

"Let him go," said Hiromy, stepping in front of Falcon.

Falcon threw Laars to the wall.

Laars smiled and wiped off the drips of juice that had spilled on his suit. "See you around, traitor."

A frowning Hiromy stood before him. "Ignore him. I'm the one who is talking to you right now."

Falcon forced his attention to Hiromy. "Yes?"

"Where do you think you're going?"

Falcon remained quiet.

She brought her hands to her hips. "I asked you a question."

"I was going anywhere that wasn't here," said Falcon thickly. "You heard your dad. He doesn't believe the Suteckh are planning to attack Ladria. I failed at convincing him. What other reason do I have to be here?"

Hiromy's eyes became glossy. "So that's why you invited me? You used me to get close to my dad?"

"No. It's not like that."

"That's exactly how it is! I thought you were different. But you're just like everyone else. You just want to use me for your own personal reasons." A tear escaped her eye.

"I'm so sorry, Hiromy," said Falcon, feeling like the biggest lowlife in the world. "But there are bigger things at stake than you and me right now."

Hiromy stared into his eyes. "Just go."

"Fine. I'll go." He walked around the shaky Hiromy and toward the double doors.

95

Suddenly there was a loud gasp behind Hiromy. Falcon looked just in time to see Laars spill his drink on Faith's dress. He then leaned over in her ear and whispered something to her as he took hold of her hand.

Faith pulled her hand back.

"Let's go," insisted Laars.

"I said no."

Laars' gang stood behind him, grinning.

"Any other girl would kill to be in my private quarters, sneered Laars. "You're just a bitc—"

Before he could finish his accusation, Falcon punched Laars across the jaw.

Laars staggered back. Before he could fall, Falcon picked him up over his shoulder and slammed him through a table. Pieces of drumsticks, cake, and blueberries took to the air. A second later they landed on the pristine tile, scattering across the floor.

The music stopped. Everyone in the room froze.

"How dare you touch me!" raged Laars. Blood dripped from his lower lip.

"Don't you ever call her that again!"

"Wow, what a bloody hero," said Laars, picking himself up. "Coming to the aid of everyone. Well, where were you when your brother murdered the council, including my grandfather? Where were you when your best friend betrayed you and went on a killing spree?"

Falcon stood shocked. How did Laars know so many details about Lao?

"That's right," said Laars, noticing the surprise in Falcon's face. "Everyone knows that your friend joined the Suteckh. I knew he was trash. Just like you."

Falcon grabbed Laars by the shirt. "You better watch your mouth."

"Enough," boomed the emperor. "Falcon Hyatt. You will leave my palace at once. I have had more than enough of your childish antics."

"Excuse me, sir—"

"Falcon," said Hiromy, standing beside the emperor. Her eyes were still glassy, but the tears had been wiped away. "You heard my dad. Get out of here."

Falcon let go of Laars, who now had a satisfied grin on his lips. He took a look at all the disapproving glances around him and turned toward the door.

"Wait for me, Falcon," Faith called.

Falcon stood confused as Faith walked over to Laars.

Laars seemed just as confused as Falcon.

Faith bent her knees in a curtsy. "Thank you for the night, Laars." There was no remorse or sarcasm in her voice. "Please tell your grandmother goodbye for me."

That's when Falcon saw something he'd never seen before. Laars' smug grin had disappeared. A frown formed on his face as he faced the floor.

If Falcon didn't know any better, he would have sworn that Laars was actually ashamed of himself.

CHAPTER 9

A cold chill travelled through the air as both water wielders walked across the stone floor. Their footsteps echoed loudly.

The sign that hung above the butcher shop squeaked loudly as the wind beat against it.

Chonsey's eyes darted from the sign to the dark alley. "You hear that? I think someone's following us."

"Relax, said Aya. "No one is following us."

"Y...yes," Chonsey stuttered. "I'm sure no one is." His eyes continued to wander. "But maybe we should hurry. Walking around the city at midnight is not safe."

"We'll be at your home in a few minutes."

Chonsey rubbed his hands together. "We shouldn't have stayed so long at the dance."

Aya's frustration rose. "Chonsey. Relax."

Chonsey remained quiet as they moved past the council chambers, in front of the gargoyle statues, and under the pine trees of the training fields.

"So what are you planning to do now that Emperor Romus didn't listen?" asked Chonsey.

"I don't know," said Aya. "I'll have to talk with Falcon tomorrow and see if we can figure something out."

"I could talk to my dad," said Chonsey. "He is the general of the army, after all. Maybe I could get him to listen."

"I doubt it. No offense, but your father is very hardheaded."

Chonsey stared down at the ground as he walked. "No offense taken. You're right. He can be quite stubborn."

"He's a good man, though," said Aya, worried that she might have hurt her friend's feelings. "He just wants the best for you."

"More like he wants me to be just like him. But I can't. I'm a disappointment to him. I can see it in his face every day."

She stopped in front of the mansion she called home. "Don't worry about living up to his expectations. Live up to yours and you'll be fine."

"Thanks," said Chonsey. "Well, you're home now. I'll see you tomorrow."

Aya wasn't listening. Instead she stared at the mansion from behind the black gates.

"What's wrong?" asked Chonsey.

"All the lights are off."

"Your father and mother are at the dance, are they not? It's natural that the lights would be off."

"No. My mother fell ill. She stayed at home resting. There's something wrong. She always has a candle lit at night."

"Maybe she just forgot," said Chonsey.

A sensation of dread traveled down her spine. "No, that's impossible. She has lit a candle every night since I was a little girl."

Aya opened the gate and marched inside. Chonsey followed. She tried to run as fast as she could, but the front yard was gigantic, and her dress slowed her down.

"She's probably just out—" A strange choking sound cut him off.

Aya stopped dead in her tracks.

"What was that?" Chonsey asked, his voice shaky. "It sounded like it came from the back of the mansion."

"That's where the servant cabins are." She took off toward the back.

"We should head back and find the royal guard," said Chonsey.

"You go back if you want. I'm not." She turned the corner and her heart stopped. Two unmoving guards lay on the ground. Their eyes were rolled back. A dark slime burrowed out of their mouths.

"Aren't those your parents' personal guards?" asked Chonsey.

"This can't be," said Aya, recognizing Linius and Kerone. She leaned down and inspected the slime.

"What is it?" asked Chonsey.

She rubbed the thick black liquid between her fingers. A putrid stench caused her nose to wrinkle. "I've seen this attack before. Back in Asturia the poison wielder, Cidralic, used it."

"I thought you said he died."

"He did die. I witnessed it myself."

"Where is she?" demanded a sudden rough growl. Aya couldn't discern whether it belonged to a man or a woman. "I know this be Aya Nakatomi's home. Tell me where she be."

Aya ran toward the voice. She dashed past the servant cabins and toward the grassy fields. Her heart dropped to her stomach as her eyes settled on her mom. She lay cowering on the ground. Her dirt-caked nightgown had been ripped in half. A hunched creature stood over her.

"I will never tell you," said her mom, defiantly, though she could not mask the layer of fear in her voice. "So you might as well kill me now."

The creature seemed all too willing to satisfy her wish. It lifted its muscular hand and rolled it into a fist.

Aya walked into the open. "Looking for me?" It probably wasn't the best idea, but she needed to get the creature's attention away from her mother.

The creature twisted its neck to face her.

Aya staggered back a step. It wasn't a creature, not entirely at least. It was a woman. She had untamed orange hair on her head. Her skin was a strange combination of black and brown. Thick veins were clearly visible through her muscular arms and legs, which were easy to see since she wore a sleeveless brown tunic and short pants.

"At last we meet, Aya Nakatomi." The woman stomped forward. She used her two front hands to walk, much like a gorilla. A giant hunch burst from her back, which made it seem like her face was somewhere where her neck should be. "Do yer know who I be?"

"Should I?"

The woman beat her chest and growled like an animal. She stared at Aya with bloodshot eyes as she stomped toward her. "I be Dokua. Yer might not be knowing me, but I'm sure yer knew my baby brother, Cidralic."

Baby brother? Aya had a hard time believing that. Cidralic had been a massive knight who easily stood over twelve feet tall.

"Oh yes," the woman growled. "I can see it in yer eyes that yer knew him." Her voice was rough and coarse. "Yer killed him. Didn't you? And now yer going to pay the price. Me, Dokua, will be inflicting the same pain on yer that yer have forced upon me."

"I didn't want to kill him. But your brother was evil. He killed—"

"Shut up," roared Dokua. "Enough talk. Now yer will pay."

Aya's mom jumped on Dokua's neck. "Leave her alone!"

Dokua grabbed Aya's mom and slammed her back to the ground. The massive woman brought her muscular arms over the noblewoman, ready to crush her where she lay.

Aya quickly formed two whips of water and shot them at Dokua. The water snakes wrapped themselves around her large forearms. It took Aya's full might to pull Dokua back.

"Yer want to play? Fine, let's play." The water around Dokua's forearms changed into a green color. The green quickly raced down the water whips toward Aya.

She had seen something similar before. When she fought Cidralic, he had changed one of her water creatures by inserting poison into it. It seemed Dokua was doing the same.

Aya dissolved the water whips.

Dokua laughed. "What's wrong? Not a fan of my poison, are yer?"

A sudden burst of water hit Dokua between her eyes. The weak water attack dripped to the floor.

"Yer!" Dokua stared a hole into Chonsey. "How dare yer be interfering?" She shot forward. Chonsey wielded two gusts of water. Dokua muscled through them with little effort. She slammed her shoulder into Chonsey's chest. He fell to the ground unconscious.

Before Dokua could inflict more damage on him, Aya brought her hands together. "Water discs." She moved forward while shooting flats discs of water through the air. The discs hit Dokua's face, pushing her back.

The woman growled. "Yer pack quite a punch for such a little thing. But yer attacks be mere child's play for a master poison wielder." She held her hand up, showing off her deep green emblem on the dorsal side of her glove. She blew her nose and a yellow mist emerged from it.

Poison mist! Aya instantly formed two thick igloos of ice, one around her mother and the other around Chonsey. She then wielded a water bubble around her head.

She could breathe safely, but the mist made it impossible to see. She darted her head back and forth, but all she heard was Dokua's laughter.

Swooosh!

A sudden fist slammed into her face. Aya remained on her feet. She strained herself forward, trying to hear anything out of the norm.

Swooosh!

Aya sidestepped the attack that whiffed past her head. But Dokua's other fist dug into her ribs. Aya fell to one knee.

Swooosh!

Swooosh!

This time Aya flipped over both attacks. She hit the ground and rolled toward her enemy. She landed behind Dokua. Her hands wrapped around her thick waist.

"How did yer...?"

Before Dokua could finish her sentence, Aya locked her hands together. She huffed as she picked up the massive woman in a backwards suplex. Halfway through the suplex she released her breath and tossed Dokua as hard as she could.

The nearby tree crackled loudly as Dokua crashed against it. A second later she stood, gritting her stained teeth.

Most of the mist had dissolved by now. Aya reached around her waist and pulled out the thick blue sticks. With a press of a button the sticks turned into her trusty blue batons. With a baton in each hand, she took a readied stance.

Dokua went in for another punch. Aya blocked it with her baton. She skidded backwards but maintained her block. She dug the tip of her second baton into Dokua's stomach. Aya felt as if she had just slammed her baton into a rock.

Dokua grinned and wrapped her gigantic hand around Aya's neck. She picked her up into the air. Aya struggled to break free, but Dokua's grip was too strong. Aya flipped her baton in her hands so the backside was forward. She dug both ends into the poison wielder's eyes.

"Aaarghh," screamed Dokua, releasing her grip on Aya. "Yer little bit–"

"Temper, temper," said Aya with a smirk. "You might be built like a rock, but even rocks can be broken."

Dokua flashed her fangs. She opened her mouth, and a long blistered tongue rolled out. The tongue slammed into the ground.

Aya looked on in disgust.

As the poison wielder walked, the tongue dragged behind her. She suddenly swung her head. The tongue shot forward.

Aya wielded a slab of ice. The tongue crashed into it. The ice held.

The tongue rolled back into the mouth. A second later it drove forward again. This time it crashed through the ice. It wrapped around Aya's legs and pulled her forward. In mere seconds Aya found herself in an imposing shadow.

Dokua released her grip and brought her hands down.

Aya backflipped out of the way. In the process she kicked her foe across the jaw.

Dokua grabbed Aya by her leg and flung her down.

Aya flipped back up before hitting the ground.

Both wielders stared at each other with fire in their eyes.

Claps echoed in the air. "Impressive. Very impressive."

Aya looked up.

A slim man stood above a floating slab of stone. Besides short pants, he wore no clothing. His skin was a deep brown color. Red marks were etched deep throughout his body. They somewhat resembled lightning marks. "I've never seen anyone survive more than two attacks from Dokua."

Aya ignored the compliment. "Who are you? And what are you doing in my home?"

The man bowed. "Where are my manners? I'm Kaidoz. The most powerful earth wielder you will ever see. And the left hand to the serene ruler of the Suteckh Empire, The Blood Empress."

"I thought Draknorr was her left hand," said Aya, thinking back to the dark knight.

Kaidoz grinned from ear to ear. "That fool is her right hand."

"Left or right. I couldn't care less. What business do you have here?"

"Kaidoz!" growled Dokua. "What yer be doing?"

"Forget her," said Kaidoz, pointing at Aya. "She dueled Cidralic, but she didn't kill him. The one who killed your brother was a holy wielder known as Faith."

"Aaaarrghhhh!" Dokua stared at Aya. Drool dripped from her mouth. "Tell me, water wielder. Where be this Faith?"

"She's not your concern. I'm your enemy."

"Fine. I'll beat it out of yer."

"No, you will not," said Kaidoz. "The Blood Empress requires our presence elsewhere."

"I don't care about yer Blood Empress!" roared Dokua. "I'm here for my revenge!"

"And you shall have it. That water wielder is strong-willed. She will never tell you where to find the one you seek. But if you follow the Blood Empress' orders, she will reveal the location of the holy wielder to you."

"She better." With a single leap she landed on the rock where Kaidoz stood.

Kaidoz bowed to Aya once again. "Until we meet again, my lady." The earth slab flew out into air. Aya followed it with her eyes for a moment, but in seconds it disappeared into the night sky.

CHAPTER 10

"Were you injured?" asked Falcon as he stood in the painted room, awaiting the arrival of Grandmaster Zoen. Aya and Sheridan were there as well.

"No," said Aya. "My mother is also fine. She was a little shaken, but she didn't suffer any injuries."

"How about Chonsey?"

"He needed a few stitches. But he'll be fine."

The grandmaster suddenly appeared at the door. He slowly entered. A sweet aroma followed him as he puffed away at his long pipe. "You said there were two of them?"

"Yes," answered Aya. "One was a poison wielder. The other was an earth wielder. He called himself Kaidoz."

The old grandmaster nodded as he took a seat behind his oak wood desk. "General Kaidoz is dangerous. He wields a basic element, but he's taken earth wielding to levels only the Golden Wielder could surpass. You must exercise great caution when confronting him."

"I could take him," said Sheridan. "I'm a space wielder. No earth wielder can beat me."

"I like your enthusiasm, Mr. Calhoun. But it takes much more than that to defeat a master." Zoen turned to Aya. "Did they say what they were after?"

"Yes," said Aya, her voice strained. "The poison wielder, Dokua, seeks revenge for her brother's death. She wants Faith."

"What!" said Falcon, his nerves shaken. It was bad enough that Faith had a chaos wielder hunting her, now she also had to deal with a poison wielder?

"Calm yourself, Mister Hyatt," said the grandmaster. "Panicking will not help the situation. Besides, we have more important matters to attend to."

"Faith's life is important," Falcon countered.

"Of course, but we must keep our perspective open to everything that is going on around us. We have received a mission request from Sugiko. There is a young woman who claims to be the rightful heir to the crown. You will go and investigate."

Falcon couldn't believe what he was hearing. Zoen was the only person in Ladria who believed the Suteckh were a threat, and instead of doing something about it, he was sending them on a useless mission.

"But, grandmaster," Falcon said. "This isn't the time for missions. We need to warn the other capital cities of the incoming Suteckh attack."

Zoen smiled, creating an uncountable number of wrinkles across his face. "I agree completely. But don't forget that you're still a Rohad mercenary, and as such are expected to go out on missions. That is why officially I'm sending you three to Sugiko."

"Are you saying two of us should go to Sugiko, while one of us goes to warn the capital cities?" asked Falcon.

"I would never say that. I am obliged by my position to order you to fulfill our contract." The grandmaster grinned from ear to ear. "Of course Rohad mercenaries are given freedom to fulfill their missions as they see fit, provided they don't break the law. No one will follow you around to make sure you all go to Sugiko."

Falcon smiled, feeling a much deeper respect for the ancient man than he'd ever felt before.

They instantly left the painted room and got their belongings ready.

"Be safe," said Aya, taking his hand.

Falcon returned the handshake. "I'll miss you too. Be extra cautious."

They had decided that Aya and Sheridan would head to Sugiko to fulfill the mission, while he and Faith would head over to Missea to warn them of the incoming attack. But now he wasn't sure that was the best idea. He hated the thought of not being there to protect her.

"Don't worry about me," said Aya, noticing the worry in his face. "I can take care of myself."

Falcon nodded. "I'll see you soon." He jumped into the carriage.

The inside of the carriage had dark wooden seats, soft padded walls, and an opening on each side. It was large, with enough space for four people, though at the moment Falcon and Faith were the only passengers.

He moved the thick curtain aside and waved goodbye to Aya.

"Be careful," she shouted, waving back at him. He continued to wave until the carriage turned the corner and he lost sight of her.

"Don't worry," said Faith. "Aya is the strongest girl I have ever met. She can look out for herself. Believe in her, like she believes in you."

Faith's words dissolved some of Falcon's nerves. "We've been friends ever since we were kids. I already lost Lao. I don't think I could handle losing her, too."

Faith smiled. "You won't."

Falcon stared at the girl. He knew she blamed herself for the villagers Shal-Volcseck had killed, including his own parents. He imagined it also couldn't be easy to know two psychotic wielders were after her. Yet, she appeared as serene as ever.

"How do you do it?" Falcon asked.

"How do I do what?"

"How do you remain so calm? Yesterday, for example, when Laars spilled his drink on you, you didn't seem angry.

Most girls I know would have gone ballistic if someone had done something like that."

"Getting angry wouldn't have helped. I can't control what Laars does or doesn't do. But I can control how I react to it. From now on I'll just have to avoid him."

"I can't do that. Seeing what he did made me so angry. I thought I was going to explode."

She caressed her hair. "We each have our own unique ways of dealing with stress. Maybe next time you feel like you're losing control, you should think of something soothing."

"The Ghost Knight told me to think of people I care about when I get angry, to use them as barriers. I tried it when I ran into Shal-Volcseck back at Sandoria. But that didn't work. You saw how I began to change into that...that thing. The chaos element inside is too strong to control."

"Have you ever been able to control your anger?" she asked.

"Yes, one time. When I fought Lao I was at the brink of defeat. I only managed to beat him because I composed myself with a thought."

"Wow! Really? Who did you think about? Your mom?"

Falcon staggered back, surprised by Faith's sudden giddiness.

"Well?" she said after Falcon failed to produce an answer.

He remained quiet, struggling to find the right words. How could he tell her that the thoughts of her and Aya were the only things that had saved him when he fought Lao?

Falcon cleared his scratchy throat. "Well. I was thinking. Yes. Thinking of—"

The carriage suddenly stopped.

Falcon allowed himself to breathe.

The door opened and two men boarded the carriage. One was young and skinny; the other was old and heavy.

"I'm Father Lucien. Good morning," said the large, bald man, taking a seat in front of Falcon and Faith. His large purple robe gave him the appearance of a priest. He had beady eyes and thick red lips.

"Good day to you, sir," responded Faith with her usual smile. "Nice to meet you."

Falcon settled for a much simpler, "Hello."

The skinny man eyed Falcon from top to bottom and extended his hand. "I'm Lakirk, son of the mayor of K'vitch. I'm glad you're on your way there. It's about time some professionals took a look into the disappearances."

"We have no business in K'vitch," said Falcon. "We're only passing by on our way to Missea."

Lakirk grimaced. "That is troubling news."

"Excuse me," said Faith. "What disappearances do you speak of?"

115

"It is the reason I'm headed to K'vitch now," said Father Lucien. "Children have been disappearing for the last two months. One moment they head off to sleep, the next they're never seen again. I'm hoping I can shed some light on the situation."

"With all due respect to you, Father Lucien," Lakirk said, "my father is mistaken. In order to get to the bottom of this we need real warriors, not more unanswered prayers."

Lucien smiled. "Don't be so quick to dismiss the power of prayer, my son."

The mayor's son waved his hands dismissively. "I don't have time to listen to this rubbish. I wasted enough time coming here to collect you at Father's request." He motioned at Falcon. "What we need is a professional Rohad, like him."

"Not everything can be solved with violence," countered Father Lucien.

Lakirk scratched his forehead and yawned. "I've heard enough of your sermons, Father. I'm going to sleep." He leaned against the wall and closed his eyes.

"To have so many children go missing." Faith gasped. "That's terrible."

The priest nodded. "Yes, indeed it is. The situation is arduous, but not as arduous as the walk of life."

"Er…um. Yes," mumbled Falcon.

"You're a priest?" Faith asked.

"Yes indeed I am. Father Lucien is my name. But my friends call me Father Lucien."

"You just said the exact same thing," said Falcon.

"Did I? The same things in life are only the exact same thing when they are not different." The man stared at Falcon as if awaiting an answer.

Wow. This guy is crazy. Best to ignore him.

When he got no answer from Falcon, the father turned to Faith. "Once I settle in K'vitch, I will aid the children by teaching them. This way I'll be close to them and can perhaps see what is causing the disappearances, and I'll be able to tutor them. They are in dire need of some formal education."

"Oh, you're also a teacher?" asked Faith "I also teach. Well, I did. Back when I was in Asturia."

The man nodded again. "There is always a time to teach. Whether young or old, teaching leads to learning and learning leads to teaching. Wouldn't you agree, young man?"

"Sure, why not?" said Falcon.

"One shouldn't answer when not sure. Uncertainty leads to disaster."

Falcon's frustration jumped a few levels. Why couldn't people just speak clearly?

"Quick to anger, I see. That is not good. We at the priesthood have found a simple way to overcome such anger without fail."

Falcon was suddenly interested. "Really? Tell me." The man was frustrating, but he seemed carefree. Perhaps there was a secret to this.

The man leaned forward between him and Faith, as if he were about to divulge a classified secret. "In order to control your anger, you must move forward with your head turned to the back. Learn from it. It might have lasted forever a lifetime ago, but now it slips through your fingers."

Falcon looked at the man in confusion. "What? I don't even know what to say to that. What does that even mean?"

"That's beautiful," said Faith. "I couldn't agree more."

Falcon turned to Faith with his mouth wide open. "You understood that gibberish?"

"Of course. Why wouldn't I?"

Falcon went numb. Am I really this thick?

"I can see you're a very bright young lady," said the father. "But I'd appreciate it if you were to not explain the riddle to your friend. Like many situations in life, one must sometimes work through tribulations on our own."

"Of course, Father Lucien," said Faith. "You have my word."

Falcon leaned on the soft carriage walls and closed his eyes. The father and Faith continued their conversation as Falcon dozed off. The soft clack of the horses' hooves against the dirt path was surprisingly soothing. In no time Falcon fell fast asleep.

"Everyone out!" yelled the carriage master. "We have reached K'vitch." Falcon opened his eyes. Faith remained asleep, head resting on his shoulder.

Falcon gently tapped her elbow. "Hey. We're here." Faith opened her eyes, and for a second Falcon found himself lost in the mesmerizing color of emerald.

"What?" asked Faith, her cheeks turning a soft pink.

"Oh, nothing," Falcon quickly mumbled.

Father Lucien stepped out. He moved with the grace of a wild boar, slamming and crushing Falcon as he moved, wearing a smile on his face all the while. As soon as he got out, the carriage popped up six inches. He held out his hand for Faith and helped her out. He didn't bother to do the same for Falcon.

"It was nice to meet you, Faith," said Father Lucien. "Once you're done with your mission I would love to have a missionary like you. Come look for me in the Temple of Ladria. Tell them I sent you."

"Thank you, sir. It was a great pleasure to meet you as well."

The father turned to Falcon, whispering in his ear, "Ironic that one who doesn't enjoy riddles, riddles himself." The father gazed at Faith, then back at Falcon. "Sooner or later, we must all choose what we really want in our life. Or who we want. The heart cannot wholly belong to more than one."

Falcon remained quiet. He'd had enough of trying to solve Father Lucien's riddles.

The father smiled and walked away, singing loudly to himself.

Falcon turned to Faith. Her eyes twinkled as she stared at the village.

The village looked like something out of a painting. It was surrounded on all sides by green hills, two of which had stone temples atop them. The cabins in the village were small, but beautiful. They all were made of fine logs, with dark wooden roofs. Every cabin had a small patch of flowers in front of it. The local pub even had vines dangling out of its windows.

Falcon couldn't recall K'vitch looking so alive the last time he'd visited.

"Hey!" he called to a little girl who ran in front of him with a string of flowers on her hand. She had dirt on her face and hair. Both her ponytails were a mess. "What's going on here?"

"Why, the festival of flowers, of course," said the girl as if the festival was common knowledge. "We celebrate it each year, to bring peace to the world."

"With all the disappearances going on lately, is it really a good idea to be celebrating?"

The girl shrugged. "I don't know, mister. I don't make the rules. But what I do know is my way around this here town. If there is anywhere you need to go, I can be your guide."

"Perfect," said Falcon. "We need to find the local inn."

The girl held out her hand. "Thanks won't fill my stomach, mister."

Falcon searched his pockets and came out with a gold coin. He held it inches away from the girl's begging hands. "Show us the fastest way there."

The girl jumped at the opportunity. "For a gold coin? Sure, follow me!"

Falcon and Faith followed the girl through the stone paths of the village. They stopped for a second to admire a group of women who performed a beautiful lullaby at the center of the village, then kept on moving.

"Here we are." The peasant girl pointed at a blue painted cabin. "Gsa's Inn. The owner is the nicest woman in K'vitch. Her prices are the best as well."

"Thanks." Falcon handed over the piece of gold.

The girl took the gold piece with a giant grin on her face. "Will you be attending the festival at sundown? It will be a lot of fun."

"No," Falcon said. "We will get a quick rest and be on our way."

"Oh, well, see you around." The girl tucked the coin in her pocket and dashed away.

Falcon and Faith checked in and got their room. Falcon tried to get a room with two beds, but those were all taken.

"I'm sorry," said Gsa. She had long red hair, white skin, and a pointed chin. "Many people are visiting because of the festival of flowers. I only have one room available and, as I said, it's a one-bed room."

Falcon sighed. "If there's nothing else, we'll take it."

Gsa handed Falcon a bronze key. "Upstairs, last door on the right."

"Thanks," said Falcon, taking the key. He and Faith went up the stairs and down the long corridor.

"These people love to decorate. Even the walls are full of flower decorations."

"They sure do," answered Falcon. He opened the door and walked into the small room. It was simple, just a small bed in the corner and a wooden drawer beside it. Beads of red and white flowers hung from the ceiling.

"You take the bed," said Falcon. "I'll sleep on the floor."

"Are you sure?" asked Faith.

"Of course. I can sleep anywhere. It's part of my training."

"Thanks, then." Faith threw herself on the bed and spread her arms. "I like it here. It reminds me a lot of Asturia."

"Yes it does. Especially with all the flowers."

"I would love to see the festival. Do you think there will be dancing?"

122

"I suppose so. Why do you ask? Don't tell me you also like to dance."

"Of course I love to dance. It's so liberating." Faith got up and twirled in place. "I have this dream to one day dance in front of a crowd of onlookers. Like the princesses from all those fairy tales we heard as children." She threw herself on the bed. "Don't tell me that you don't like to dance."

"No, not much. Aya use to drag me to every dance Rohad held back when we were students. My legs would always be killing me the next day." Falcon thought back to all those nights with blisters on his feet and grimaced. Though he had to admit that he would love to go back to the days where a dance was his biggest problem.

Faith giggled. "Well, you won't have to worry. We'll be out of here by then, right?"

"Yes, we will." Falcon gazed out the window. The sun was right above him. "Listen. I have go check on something. I'll be back. You should get some rest."

"Good idea. I had just dozed off in the carriage when we arrived." Falcon wasn't surprised. She had probably spent most of the trip talking to Father Lucien. Falcon was just glad he was asleep most of the trip and didn't have to deal with him.

"I'll wake you up when it's time to go," said Falcon, walking out the door.

~~~

123

Faith felt a soft tap on her leg. She sat up and rubbed her eyes. Falcon stared back at her.

"Is it time to go?" she asked.

"Sort of." He grinned. "C'mon, follow me."

"What do you mean, sort of?"

"You'll see. Just come downstairs."

"Fine." Faith was intrigued. Why is he acting so mysterious all of a sudden?

"Close your eyes," said Falcon, just as they reached the inn door. "No peeking."

Faith did as Falcon said and closed her eyes. She was tempted to peek, but fought the urge. Falcon grabbed her hand and led her forward. The door creaked loudly as Falcon opened it. The soothing breeze coursed through her hair as she moved outdoors.

"You can open your eyes now," said Falcon.

"Happy Flowers Day, Faith!" yelled the crowd of strangers.

Faith's heart jumped. The peasant girl handed her a bouquet of pink and orange cream-colored flowers.

Falcon walked to the middle of the crowd of people and extended his hand. "I feel partially guilty for the horrible dance you had the other day. Let me make it up to you. May I have this dance?"

Feeling strangely nervous, she took his hand. The group of female singers she'd seen earlier sang a slow melody. It was just like her dream.

"But I thought we had to leave tonight?" she asked.

"It turns out the road to Missea is currently obstructed by a rockslide. There's no way across until it gets cleared tomorrow morning. I thought we might as well make the best of it."

Butterflies fluttered inside of her. "How did you ever get everyone to do this?"

"It wasn't too hard. The people of this village are really friendly. Too friendly if you ask me."

"Thank you." She looked up at the stars. Their radiant light seemed to be shining just for her. Everything was perfect.

She knew that there was danger around her. The Suteckh were launching an attack on Va'siel. And both Shal-Volcseck and Dokua were searching for her. But tonight, just for one night, she allowed herself to forget her problems as she rested her head on her friend's chest and moved to the music.

Chapter 11

"Once Hyatt left Hiromy stranded at the party, I swooped in like the gentleman I am," bragged Sheridan as they walked along the dirt path. He dragged his feet, which lifted a storm of dust. "I took her dancing, and we spoke all night. She actually sounded interested in me."

"That's great," said Aya.

"So what do you think I should do now? Should I play it cool? Or should I just tell Hiromy how I've felt about her for the past five years?"

"I'm not sure." Aya shrugged. "I really don't know her well enough to give you any good advice. But I do know one thing: at this rate you're going to suffocate me with all that dust you're leaving behind. Please walk properly."

He straightened his posture and lifted his feet. "I think I'm going to take it slow. She's bound to like that."

"If you say so," said Aya, trying to concentrate. The trees and bushes around them were the perfect place for an ambush.

"Would you relax, Nakatomi? We've have been walking for two days, and we've hardly seen any other people. If someone wanted to ambush us, they would have done so by now."

"Sheridan," said Aya, trying to sound as polite as possible. "Could you please keep it down? I'm trying to listen."

"Listen to what?" asked Sheridan. He stopped humming. "There's nothing to hear. No birds singing, no other travelers, and no sound of any woodland critters."

"Exactly. That's what has me worried." Aya strained her ears, trying to hear something - anything. But even the sound of the wind was absent.

Her head suddenly grew hazy, and her body weakened. She tapped her head, trying to regain her senses.

"My hands and legs feel weak," said Sheridan, wobbling from side to side.

"Move back!" cried Aya as she noticed the brown blur coming down on them.

The net swept up from under Sheridan's feet and picked him up into the air.

Dozens of slim dark-clad figures dropped from the trees. Their faces were painted with elaborate patterned designs. They all wore black suits from head to neck.

The ground trembled as a large figure landed before her. He towered over her small figure. Red lines were etched on his cheeks. Dark lines also ran around his gigantic arms and legs. Save for a long leather skirt, he wore no armor.

"Get away," said Aya, taking a step back. "I don't want to hurt any of you. Just let my friend go and we won't have a problem."

The large man remained quiet.

"And how exactly do you plan to do that?" jeered a high-pitched feminine voice. "There's two of you and fifteen of us. And your idiot friend over there is hanging from his feet."

"Hey!" complained Sheridan. "I may be an idiot, but I more than make up for it with my amazing fighting skills, my witty comments, and my dashing good looks." He smiled, revealing a set of pearly white teeth.

A short girl, who looked to be about twelve, emerged from the crowd of men. She had long, dark eyes, tiny lips, and two lines of red paint running vertically on her cheeks. "We'll see just how funny ya are after Keira is done with you. She loves putting jokers in their place."

"Mmmmm," said Sheridan tantalizingly. "It sounds like me and this Keira could have great fun together. But, alas, I'll have to pass. For my heart belongs to another. Please relay your message to your frisky leader."

Aya rubbed her temple. How could he be jesting at a time like this?

"Just let me do the talking," said Aya. She faced the crowd. "I'll tell you one more time: let me go or else."

The large man acted as if she hadn't even spoken. He walked up to the net and cut the rope with a knife he pulled from his scabbard. Sheridan crashed to the ground.

"That's it!" cried Sheridan. He waved his arms in grandiose fashion. "Feel the power of space pressure." Nothing happened.

"We have to get out of here!" exclaimed Aya, realizing that Scaiths were nearby. It was the only explanation for Sheridan's wielding being nullified. "The creatures that can suppress wielding are close. We're all in great danger."

Except for the large man, the group of attackers burst out in laughter.

Maybe they don't understand me. She recalled Faith mentioning that most people knew Scaiths by their other name—devourers.

"The devourers are coming," said Aya, hoping that the attackers would now understand the urgency of the situation.

The attackers laughed even harder than before. Some cackled so loudly that they were having a hard time breathing.

What could possibly be so funny? mused Aya.

The small girl pointed the sharp end of the spear at Aya's head. "Shut up and get moving or yar idiot friend here gets it."

Aya took a breath and put her hands down in defeat. She would have to play along for now and do as she was told.

The large man threw Sheridan over his shoulder and began to walk.

Aya followed close behind. In her mind she analyzed dozens of escape plans, but in none of them was she able to formulate an idea where Sheridan wasn't left behind. The fact that she had no wielding made this even harder.

"Ya have ugly hair," said the girl as she ran circles around her, her short brown hair dancing behind her. She then stopped and stared at her. "Ya also have a stupid face. Not like Keira. She's much more beautiful than ya."

Aya didn't answer.

The girl's brown eyes stared back at her as she continued to throw her insults. "How were ya planning to beat us? Ya don't even have any weapons."

"I don't only rely on weapons. I'm also a martial artist."

"Ha," snickered the girl. "Keira is also a martial artist. I bet she could destroy ya in a duel. You'll be no match for her. She's the best in Sugiko."

"Rika!" called the large man without turning around. "Quit fraternizing with the prisoner."

"I'm not fraternizing, Raji. I was merely telling this loser the truth."

"Quiet," ordered Raji.

Rika murmured something under her breath and stomped to the back of the line, but not before sticking her tongue out at Aya.

They walked for what seemed ages. They went up a mountain and back down to a large valley. The sun was close to setting when they finally arrived at a wooden gate. The gate ran in a circle. Raji knocked three times on the door, whistled twice, and then knocked two more times.

"Who goes there?" said a voice from the other side of the gate.

"It is I, Raji of the Minotaur clan."

There was the sound of wood blocks being removed. Then the gate opened.

Dozens of leather tents were spread throughout the camp. Hundreds of people gathered around small campfires. Their clothes were ragged and streaked with dirt.

A girl, who looked to be around Aya's age, marched toward them. She wore a brown tunic and pants. Her golden-brown hair was tied in a ponytail and braided with pigtails.

Judging by the crowd behind her, Aya was certain this had to be the girl Rika had told her about.

"We found these people roaming close to the camp, Keira," said Rika.

"Rohads!" shrieked Keira. "Where exactly did you find 'em?"

"Traveling the emperor's road," answered Raji, dropping Sheridan to the ground.

"No doubt Hotaru hired them so they could hunt us down," added a man from the crowd. The women and men around them nodded to each other.

"Gutless Rohads," fumed Keira, tearing open Sheridan's net with a knife. "I'm going to kill you here and now."

"Are you sure that's a wise idea?" said Raji. "Perhaps it would be best to keep them as prisoners for ransom."

Keira stared coldly at Raji. "So they can eat our food? No, we are starving as it is. These two die now."

The crowd cheered and clapped.

"You, get up," said Keira, kicking Sheridan in the stomach. "Let's see how tough you are when your opponent fights back."

Opponent fights back? What is she talking about?

Sheridan stood. "I make it a point to not hit girls. Perhaps we could tangle another way." He lifted his eyebrows and smiled invitingly. A punch to the face quickly wiped it off.

"Shut up and fight, Rohad."

"Sorry, martial arts isn't really my forte," answered Sheridan. "I'm more of a swordfighter. And I'd really rather not use it. Trust me. It wouldn't end well for you."

Keira smirked. "Go ahead. Use your weapon."

Sheridan shrugged and pulled out his machete-looking sword. "Don't say I didn't warn you." He shot forward.

Keira dropped and swept her legs across the ground. Sheridan flipped over the attack.

Keira pressed both hands on the ground and used them as leverage to throw herself through the air. Sheridan's jaw cracked loudly as her feet slammed under his chin.

Sheridan staggered back. He rubbed his jaw. After a few seconds, he swung his sword again.

This time Keira caught it in her hand. At the same time she kicked the side of his head.

Sheridan crashed to the ground. He immediately flipped back up. But before he could regain his balance, Keira kicked him back down. She brought the blade to Sheridan's neck.

The crowd cheered.

"Keira, Keira, Keira!" Rika cheered louder than anyone else.

Aya could now see that Rika hadn't exaggerated. Keira's moves were flawless. Her attacks were precise and deadly. No move was wasted.

"Ready to die?" Keira threatened, pressing the blade into Sheridan's neck.

"Leave him alone," ordered Aya. "We are not here to see Hotaru. In fact, we were dispatched to fight against him."

"Lies!" Keira sneered. "Rohads are nothing but a lot of deceitful cowards."

"She said she's a better martial artist than ya, Keira," added Rika. "Mop the floor with her."

"I didn't say such a thing," said Aya.

Rika brought her hands to her hips. "Did too."

Keira stepped up to Aya so they were face to face. "Just like a Rohad to think they're better than anyone else." She spat at Aya's feet. "I'll tell you what. If you defeat me, I'll let you two go."

"And if I lose? What then? You'll kill us?"

"I was going to kill you either way. But if you lose, your death will be slow and painful."

The last thing she wanted to do was fight. Her legs ached from all the walking, and she hadn't had a morsel to eat since the morning.

Keira eyed her from head to toe. "So?"

Aya brought up her fists in a readied stance.

"Hiaaaa!" Keira shot toward her with a punch. Aya ducked under it and delivered an uppercut. Keira adjusted her weight and hopped away. Aya quickly changed formations in mid-attack and kicked into the air. Keira did the same. The girls' legs slammed into each other.

Aya brought her feet down on her opponent's head. Keira grabbed Aya's leg and drove herself under it. She then pushed up.

Aya took to the air and crashed onto the floor. Even through her ringing ears, she could hear the roar of the crowd.

Keira pressed forward.

Aya waited. At the last second she rolled out of the way. Keira's kick flew past her.

Aya grabbed her foe's leg and twisted it. At the same time she delivered an open palm strike to the forehead.

Keira screamed as she too fell to the ground.

The roar of the crowd ceased.

Keira stood. Her face was a deep red. She brought her hands together and took a deep breath. "Kyyaaa!" She attacked with untamed ferocity.

Aya did the same.

For the next few minutes both girls went all out in a series of attacks, blocks, and counters. Neither girl was able to get the upper hand.

The crowd remained silent.

Aya ducked under a kick and punched her opponent on the knee. Keira kicked Aya in the ribs as she stumbled back. Both girls fell to the ground at the same time.

Suddenly a series of loud growls pierced the air. The crowd parted as three bears, running on all fours, broke through. They reached Aya and stood on their hind legs. Drool dripped from their exposed fangs.

Shocked, Aya crawled back until she smashed into a stack of hollowed barrels.

They surrounded her. Then, with mouths open, they pounced.

CHAPTER 12

Each of the bears was a different color. One was fully black, one pure white, and the last one was a light brown. Despite their differences, all of them seemed equally intent on killing her.

"Stop this!" an older woman cried.

She emerged from the crowd. Her face was marred with countless wrinkles, and even her long nose was full of deep lines. A small wooden staff seemed to be the only thing keeping her from falling.

Keira held her hand up. The bears immediately stepped back and ceased snarling.

Is she controlling them?

"What is the meaning of this interruption, Nanake?" asked Keira. There was a layer of respect in her voice. "I am busy at the moment."

"These people are not with Hotaru. I summoned them."

"You called 'em?" Keira asked, her voice raising. "Why? What use could we have for Rohads?"

"You know why. We are severely outnumbered. We need all the help we can get."

Keira stomped her feet as she paced in a small circle. "We don't need help from 'em. We can handle this ourselves."

The elder lady spoke with determination in her voice. "No, we cannot. We have already lost half of our camp. How many more must we lose? The Rohads can help our cause. You must allow them to stay."

Keira stared at Nanake for a moment as she bit her lower lip. "Out of respect for you, I'll let this pass this once." She narrowed her eyes. "But don't forget that I'm in charge here, not you. Don't ever pull something like this again."

"So does that mean they can stay?"

"Yes. I suppose we need someone to carry our weapons in the upcoming attack." Keira turned and stormed off. The trio of bears followed after her.

"I'm sorry about that," said Nanake. "My niece is a good person. But she's been through a lot the last couple of months."

"It's fine," said Aya. She stood and dusted herself off. "She's not the first of our clients to not exactly welcome us with open arms." Images of the late Captain Benoit flashed through her mind.

"Please come with me." The old lady trudged to a raging fire at the middle of the camp, taking a seat by it. Aya and Sheridan sat beside her. "You have come at the right time. I was afraid you would not be here when we launched our attack."

"So what exactly is going on here?" asked Sheridan. "Our briefing report was very vague. Perhaps you can fill us in."

Nanake sighed. "Years ago Sugiko was a prospering capital city. My brother, Emperor Takumi, and his wife ushered us into an era of peace and prosperity." Her face turned stern. "But ten years ago the royal advisor, Hotaru, killed them in their sleep. He claimed Sugiko's throne as his own. Keira was just a little girl when it happened."

"How did she manage to survive?" asked Aya.

"I don't know. She has never spoken about that night to anyone. All I know is that she ran to the woods, where she remained for six years."

Sheridan whistled slowly. "Six years. That's a long time."

"Yes. Everyone thought she was dead," continued Nanake. "I never gave up hope and continued to search. My perseverance was rewarded four years ago. I found her living in a cave with her bears."

Aya narrowed her eyes and met the woman's gaze. Her curiosity was now at its peak. "Bears? Tell me, how is it that she can see through them?"

The woman's eyes widened. "You noticed then?"

"Noticed what?" asked Sheridan.

Aya turned to her companion. "Keira's eyes are hazy white. She had difficulty blocking low attacks, but had no problems stopping high and mid-level attacks."

Sheridan scratched his head. "So her lower defense is weak and she has white eyes, what of it?"

"She's blind, Sheridan."

"Blind?" Sheridan's face twisted in confusion. "But how can she fight so well if she can't see?"

"Because she sees through her bears." Aya faced the ancient woman. "Isn't that right?"

"Yes. But don't ask me how. I don't even know how she does it. All I know is that when we found her she already had the ability."

"B...but that makes no sense," stuttered Sheridan. "No one should be able to do that."

"That's besides the point. What matters is that my niece is the rightful ruler of Sugiko."

"She's right," said Aya. She had questions about Keira's mysterious abilities as well. But she forced her curiosity to the back of her head. She'd been tasked with aiding a princess to reclaim her throne. And that was what she intended to do.

"If what you say is true, why wait until now to reclaim the city?" Sheridan asked.

"Keira was too young. She couldn't officially lay claim to throne of Sugiko until she came of age, which she did last month, when she turned eighteen. We tried launching an attack, but more than half our force was crushed. We only have about one hundred soldiers left."

"So how do you plan to reclaim the city with so few soldiers?" questioned Sheridan.

"A distraction," answered Aya instinctively.

Nanake smiled. "I see you are quite observant. Yes, you are indeed correct. We plan to launch a diversionary attack from the front, but at the same time Keira, along with a few chosen warriors, will sneak into the royal palace. With luck, she'll end Hotaru's treachery once and for all. His men rape, terrorize, and murder the people of Sugiko in the name of security. They must all be stopped." Nanake's voice lowered to a whisper. "The mission must not fail. That is why I called on you Rohads for aid. We need the best for the upcoming battle."

Sheridan flexed his arms. "I am considered the best of the best." He put his emblem in Nanake's face. "See that? I'm a space wielder, which means I'm a beast—well, if I could wield, that is."

Aya slapped Sheridan's arm out of the way, unable to believe his nerve. "Don't be rude." She turned to Nanake. "Are there any Scaiths in the area?"

"You know about Scaiths?" asked Nanake, clearly surprised.

"We ran into one once," said Sheridan. "They have this annoying ability of suppressing the energy within a wielder, essentially making it impossible for us to use our abilities."

"Our bravest hunters hunt them for sport," said Nanake. "We discovered a way to harness the energy inside of them into a stone."

"Who would be crazy enough to hunt those things?" asked Sheridan. "They're as large as full-grown bears and have metal plates all over their body."

Aya ran her finger atop her chin, finally figuring out what was going on. "So whoever carries said stone has the ability to stop wielders from using their elemental attacks."

"I'm sorry," said Nanake, smiling. "I'm not much of an alchemist. I don't know how such a device works."

Sheridan looked from Aya to Nanake with a worried expression. "But I assume your niece will not bring the stone with her on the mission. That would only hinder our chances of success."

"I'm afraid it's not us that have the stone. It's Hotaru. He has amassed so many that wielding in Sugiko is literally impossible." She lowered her voice. "To make matters worse, he has a device that allows his soldiers to wield."

"Great. Just great," whined Sheridan. "So they can wield at us all they want, but we can do nothing."

"I don't like it either," Aya added.

Nanake did not look worried. "Young lady, after seeing your performance against my niece, I know I made the right choice. No one has ever lasted more than a few seconds against her in combat. You did, which can only mean you're the perfect person for this job."

Aya forced a smile, quietly wishing she could be as confident as Nanake.

Once the conversation was over, Aya grabbed her belongings and moved to the corner of the small camp. The men and women stared at her with curious eyes, but no one spoke.

She set out her night towel and lay atop it. She tossed and turned from side to side. Usually she wouldn't mind sleeping on the floor, but this floor was full of jagged edges.

"You're a rich girl, aren't ya?" asked Rika with a large grin. Her face paint was still on.

"What makes you say that?"

"Rika, leave the pampered rich girl be," jeered Keira, lying atop the night towel she had spread beside Aya.

"Rich, yes," Aya countered. "Pampered, no."

Keira laughed. "All you money girls are the same. The biggest problem you ever had to face was what color makeup you were going to wear. You know nothing of real pain. Not like me and my cousin, Rika."

"Stop talking," said Aya, growing agitated. "You know nothing of my life."

"I know you fight for money and nothing else. You don't understand loss. How could you? You have never lost anyone precious in your life."

Selene's smile flashed in her mind as she stood. "I told you to be quiet! Were you there when my little sister was taken from me? When she begged me for help but I was too weak to save her?"

Keira and Rika remained uncharacteristically quiet.

"Were you there when my parents asked me where Selene was and I had no answer? You want to know why I fight? It's not for money. I do it so that no girl ever again has to cry herself to sleep wondering what became of her sister. I do it so no one suffers like I have suffered, like I suffer every day." Aya's voice and body trembled.

"Aya?" mumbled Sheridan. "I had no idea."

The tips of her ears grew warm as she clutched her night towel and ran to the darkest corner of the camp, away from prying eyes. She lay down and stared at the sky, ashamed that she had allowed herself to lose control.

As she gazed at the stars, her sister's cries echoed in her ears.

"Selene. I'm sorry for failing you," whispered Aya. "I'm so sorry."

Chapter 13

Falcon opened the windows. The smell of wet dirt coursed through the air. Soft rain fell on his head and face. He looked back. Faith was still fast asleep in bed.

Falcon closed the window and picked up his sheets from the floor where he had slept. He must have made more noise than he thought, because Faith's eyes opened all of a sudden.

"Good morning," said Faith, sitting up. With her hand she pushed down the few strands of hair that were out of place. "How did you sleep last night?"

"Not bad," answered Falcon. "I'm used to sleeping in hard places."

"Why? Don't you have beds at Rohad?"

"We do, but Rohads are not only trained in battle. We never know what our mission will require of us, so we prepare for any foreseeable circumstance. Two weeks out of the year we sleep out in the open. Sometimes in the forest, desert, you name it. We have sleeping towels, of course. But it's still uncomfortable."

Faith winced. "That sounds harsh."

"It's not that bad. You get used to it after a while. Chonsey was the only one in our group who never really adjusted to sleeping outdoors. One time he even—"

A loud knock rocked the door. The tree painting crashed to the ground.

"Coming," said Falcon. The knocks came again, even louder than the first time. He quickened his pace and opened the door.

The little girl from before glared up at him. "Hello."

"Er…hello," said Falcon.

"Nice morning we're having." The girl stared back at him expectantly.

"Um…can I help you with something?"

"Oh no, not really, I suppose. I'm here to lend my services. Anything you need, I'm your girl."

"We won't be needing anything anymore. We must be on our way."

"That's impossible. The road won't be clear until midday."

Falcon brought his hand to his forehead and sighed. How much longer are we going to be slowed down for?

She smiled crookedly. "Don't feel too bad. There is an upside to everything. Now you have time to tour the village. And you're in luck. I'm the best tour K'vitch has got. I can take you and your girlfriend to the must romantic pond in Va'siel."

Falcon narrowed his eyes. "She's not my girlfriend."

"Oh, excuse me. I just assumed since you stayed in the same room and all."

"That was only because—" He stopped himself in mid sentence. Why am I explaining myself to a twelve year old?

Faith came from behind Falcon and extended her hand. "What's your name?"

"Me?" The girl pointed at herself as she took Faith's hand and shook it. "My name is Iris. You know, like the flower."

"Nice to formally meet you, Iris. I'm Faith, and this is Falcon." She bent down to the girl's level. "I'll tell you what. Since we're still stuck here, I would love a tour of the village."

"We would?" Falcon asked, surprised by Faith's offer.

"Of course. As soon as I get ready, we'll be downstairs."

Iris shot a puzzled look at Faith. "Ready? You look beautiful as it is."

Faith smiled. "Thank you, but my hair is a mess. I'll be out shortly. How much is your fee?"

"Are you kidding?" exclaimed Iris. "That gold coin you gave me will keep me fed for a month. This one is on me." She closed the door. Her loud voice traveled into the room. "I'll be waiting downstairs."

"You don't really want a tour, do you?" asked Falcon, suspecting that Faith only wanted to help the girl.

"No. But I feel bad for her. She's so young, and she's already roaming the streets by herself. Maybe there's something I can do to help."

Falcon sighed. "I want to help her as much as you, but we can't stop to aid everyone in need who gets in our way."

"I know. But you heard Iris. We're stuck here until midday. We can't go anywhere else. Unless you know a different way to Missea."

"There are different paths to Missea, but they're all too long to traverse. The mountain pass is a ten-day trip, and a sea voyage is over thirty days."

"So I guess we don't have much of a choice."

"Suppose not."

They both washed up and headed downstairs. The girl sat on a sofa that decorated the inn. A small dog rested by her feet.

Iris stood, causing the dog to whimper. "So where do you want to go first? The pond? Rosarie's palace of trinkets? Cesar Adrian's weapon shop? Grimmie's music hall?"

"Just a simple place to eat would be nice," said Falcon, putting an end to her spiel. "We haven't had breakfast yet."

"Of course, follow me." She led them out of the inn and down a stone path. The remains of the previous day's celebration remained scattered about: flower ribbons, half-empty mugs of ale, bread crumbs, and pichion bones. Half a dozen of K'vitch's citizens were hard at work tossing the trash into wooden barrels.

"Here we are," said Iris, pointing at a fine oak wood building before them. The sweet aroma of blueberry and cherry pie flowed out of the two open windows. "Lana's Stop serves the best pies and hotcakes in the village."

"It sure smells good," said Faith, licking her lips.

Falcon grabbed the overly smooth handle and held the door open.

Faith walked a few steps in and stopped. "Aren't you coming, Iris?"

The girl shrank back. "Me? Oh no. I couldn't possibly step foot in there. I've seen it through the window a few times. Everything is so nice, and I look like..." She gazed down at her dirt-caked clothes. "Well I look like this."

"It's fine," said Faith, taking the girl's hand. "You're our guest today."

With wobbly legs, Iris stepped into the restaurant. Her eyes sparkled as she gazed at the surroundings.

Falcon couldn't see why. It looked like an average dining room to him. In fact, it was less than average. A few cut logs served as chairs. The fading polish on the wooden tables showed their advanced age. The crooked paintings that hung on the walls were cracked. Even the flowers in the pot were half dead.

The commotion in the dining room died as soon as they walked in. Everyone looked at Falcon with the same hateful eyes he was used to seeing back in Ladria.

A moment later, however, he realized that they weren't looking at him. The people were looking past him, directly at Iris.

"What are you doing here?" asked a skinny mustached man, pointing at Iris. "I told you you're not welcome here. It's bad enough I always find you eating out of my trash." The man turned to Falcon and Faith. His voice changed to one of compassion. "I'm so sorry you had to stand next to this vermin. Rohads are regarded in the highest esteem by the people of K'vitch. I assure you this won't happen again."

Falcon gritted his teeth. From the corner of his eye he noticed Faith shaking her head.

The man turned his attention to Iris. "You're still here? I told you. Off with you, vermin."

A whimper escaped Iris as she stared down at the ground and turned toward the door.

Before she could walk, Faith held the girl in place and faced the man. "Her name is Iris, not vermin."

The man's eyes darted nervously from Faith to Iris.

Falcon cracked his anxious knuckles. "Iris is with us. If she goes, we go as well." He stepped in front of the man so they were face to face. "Rest assured I will report this incident back at Ladria. Your restaurant will be blacklisted from our record books."

A look of panic came over the man's face. "Please don't do that. Traveling Rohads make up over eighty percent of my

149

sales…I…I." He took a breath as he wiped the sweat that had formed in his brow. "I misspoke earlier. I'm sorry…er…"

"Her name is Iris," said Faith.

"Y…yes, Iris. You are welcome here any time you want. Let me make up for this little misunderstanding by providing your meal free of charge. Please follow me to our best table. It has a wonderful view of the pond."

"What do you say, Iris?" asked Falcon. "Do you still want to eat here? Or would you rather go somewhere else?"

The owner glanced at Iris as he played with his quivering hands.

"Here will be fine."

The man exhaled. "Please follow me."

The rest of the people stared at them with curiosity as the owner led them to a large table at the corner of the restaurant. There was a window beside it where one had a clear view of a pristine pond. Ducks paddled in circles, with their newborn ducklings following close behind.

"Colette," called the owner.

A blond woman emerged from behind the counter. "Yes."

"Bring our guests some water. Make sure it's the spring water. Nothing but the best for our three friends."

"That's more like it," said Falcon, still angry. "Now make yourself scarce."

The owner craned his neck. "Of course, sir. I'm sure you will remember my hospitality when you return to Ladria, right?"

"You're still here?" said Falcon. He turned to the girl. "Iris, will you please tell this man to get lost?"

Iris's eyes darted nervously from Falcon to the owner.

Faith rested her hand on Iris's hand. "Don't worry, honey. You don't have to say anything."

The girl took a breath, and the owner slunk away without saying another word.

Faith stared at Falcon. "You shouldn't put her on the spot like that." There was an intensity in her eyes Falcon had never seen before.

"What?" He shrugged. "He was rude to Iris. I thought she would like some payback."

"So you're going to teach her to be just like him? To humiliate other people because it's fun to get payback?"

"Faith. I was angry. I wanted him to feel what she felt."

"That's not an excuse. If the world thought that way, we would all be treating each other with disrespect and fear."

Falcon stopped talking as he pondered her words for a second. How many times was he going to let his anger control him? And now he was bringing other people into it. He had to make amends. "I'm sorry, Iris. Faith is right. I shouldn't have put you on the spot like that."

Iris didn't answer. She remained frozen in place as if she were lost in another world.

Faith waved her hands in front of the girl. "Iris, are you well?"

"Yes," said Iris. Her eyes were red and glassy. "It's just that…that no one has ever been kind to me. She buried her head in her hands. "No one has ev…er stood up for me."

Faith put her arm around Iris. "It's fine."

The spectacle both saddened and angered Falcon. He knew something of the pain Iris felt. How could someone be so cruel to a child?

Colette passed by and left three mugs at the table. She walked away without saying a word.

"Here, drink some water," said Faith, handing Iris one of the mugs.

Iris grabbed the mug and drank half its contents in one gulp. A second later, the mug slipped through Iris's fingers and crashed to the ground. A black layer formed around her eyes and lips. Her neck fell back as her eyes rolled back. Dark blood dripped from her nose. Faith caught her seconds before her limp body tumbled down.

"What's going on?" asked Falcon.

Faith glanced at Falcon with terror in her eyes. "Poison."

CHAPTER 14

Falcon turned to the owner of the restaurant. "You did this."

"Me, sir?" asked the man, pointing at himself.

"Yes, you." Falcon grabbed him by his shirt. "As soon as she drank the water you sent her, she fell ill. What kind of poison did you use? Tell me now!"

He put up his hands defensively. "I swear by my mother that I did not poison her. That water was brought to me fresh from the river this morning."

The owner sounded sincere, but Falcon didn't buy his act. Who else would have reason to poison Iris?

"Aaarrghhhh!" Iris's pained scream filled the restaurant.

"Falcon!" cried Faith. "I have never seen poison like this. I can't extract it. Every time I try it I hurt her more. We have to take her to the infirmary as soon as possible."

"This is not over yet," said Falcon, letting go of the man. "I will get to the bottom of this." He took Iris' flimsy body in his arms and carried her out. Luckily she didn't weigh much, so she was easy to run with.

"Where's the infirmary?" asked Faith. A group of people stared at her in silence.

"Where is it?" repeated Falcon.

A short woman leapt to attention. "It's not much of an infirmary, actually. But it's the best we got. It's more of a—"

Falcon pinched his lips together. "I don't need details. Just tell me where it is."

"The last building at the end of the road."

"Thank you," said Faith.

Falcon took off in a full-out sprint. The people and cabins became a jumble of blurs. He vaguely made out Faith's heavy breaths as she kept pace behind him.

Faith pointed at the old white cabin. "This is it." She knocked on the door.

Falcon paced back and forth, waiting for a response. When he looked down at Iris, his world halted. "Faith, she's really pale."

Faith took Iris's sweaty face between her hands. "Don't close your eyes." She shook her from side to side and Iris opened them. "That's it. Keep them open. You must stay awake."

Falcon moved to the door and kicked it with all his strength. The old wood splintered in a dozen places.

"Calm yourselves," came a voice from the other side. "I'm coming."

Falcon kicked again. "Hurry up!"

The door opened and Falcon came face to face with a familiar face. Father Lucien. In his hand he carried a mug of steaming red tea. He dropped it to the floor, scattering the hot contents everywhere. "Bring her in."

Falcon followed the father to an empty bed in the corner of the room. He slowly set Iris down, careful to not hurt her any further.

Father Lucien ran his hands over Iris's forehead. "What happened?"

"She's been poisoned," said Faith, her voice trembling. "But I couldn't remove the poison, even with my holy wielding."

Father Lucien shook his head. "You're a holy wielder?"

"Yes. But like I said, my wielding was not helpful."

"Well then, this is troublesome. Holy wielders are said to be the ultimate healers, and if you couldn't heal her, I don't think I'll be much help. I'm a simple part-time medic."

Falcon's eyes darted from the father to Faith. "So is there anything either of you can do? I'm sure together you can figure something out."

Father Lucien put his head over Iris's chest. "Her heartbeat is faint." He bent down and examined her face.

Falcon stepped back as dark rims appeared around Iris's eyes and mouth. He could spend an entire day in battle. But here, among healers, he was but a novice.

Father Lucien looked defeated. "The fact that the poison is appearing in dark circles suggests that it's working extremely fast. I think we only have a few minutes."

Faith closed her eyes and shook her head. Once in a while she would mutter "No" or "That won't work either."

Falcon tapped Faith's arm. "Are you—"

"Shhh…" said Father Lucien. "Can't you see she's trying to find a solution?"

"I can see a light," Iris mumbled.

Falcon's clammy hands took hold of the girl's arm. His heartbeat intensified as he shook her. "Hey. Don't go to sleep."

"We need to extract the poison," said Faith, her eyes opening.

The father shook his head. "You said you already tried that and failed. Why would it work this time?"

"Bring me the surgical tools," ordered Faith.

The father ran to a small study at the corner of the room. He opened a desk and pulled out a brown bag. Huffing loudly, he rushed back to Faith.

Falcon remained nervous and confused. "How is that going to help?"

"I'm lost too," said Father Lucien.

Faith took the bag and pulled out a long silver knife. She handed it to the father. "You're going to cut exactly where I tell you."

Father Lucien took the knife. "M…me? But I'm not even a surgeon."

"Today you are," said Faith. She ran her finger behind Iris's ear. "I want you to cut there, and only there."

"Yes," said Father Lucien. With trembling hands he set the knife where he'd been instructed.

Faith took his hand. "Calm down and wait for me to tell you when." She turned to Falcon. "I need you to hold her down. I can't have her squirming."

Falcon set his hands on Iris's shoulders and pressed down.

Faith put her hand over Iris's face and mumbled. The white emblem glowed with intensity as the dark lines around the girl's eyes moved in a snake-like manner toward the ear.

The fact that Iris didn't even flinch told Falcon how close they were to losing her. His mouth went dry at the thought.

"Now," said Faith.

Father Lucien pierced as Faith had told him. Dark blood gushed out of the cut. After a few seconds the blood turned a normal red.

Iris opened her eyes. "What happened? Where am I?"

"You're fine now," said Faith, as she covered the cut with a towel. "Lie down and rest."

Falcon Lucien stared at Faith with admiration. "You knew that you couldn't pull the blood all the way. So you gathered it in one spot and took it out with an incision. Amazing. Simply amazing."

157

"It was nothing," said Faith. "I'm just glad Iris is well."

Despite Faith's humility, Falcon couldn't help feeling proud of her. She was truly remarkable.

Faith's face turned red as her gaze met Falcon's. "Why are you looking at me that way?"

"Oh, sorry." He shook his head. "Listen. You two look over Iris. I'm going to have a talk with the owner of the restaurant. He knows something, and I'm going to get to the bottom of it."

"Yes," said Faith, "but you heard him. He said he didn't have anything to do with the poisoning."

"Of course he said that. But who else could it have been? It has to be him."

"I'm not too sure," Faith insisted. "I'm pretty good at telling when people are lying, and the man seemed truthful."

Falcon wasn't convinced. "I guess we'll find out, won't we?" As he reached for the handle, the door swung open.

A boy stumbled in. "Help me!" He had the same dark lines around his eyes and mouth. He was pale and sweat dripped from his hair. "Please…" The boy collapsed. Falcon caught him before he fell to the ground. With the help of Father Lucien, he set him on one of the empty beds.

"What did you drink or eat?" asked Falcon.

"He's passed out," said Father Lucien as he listened for the boy's heartbeat.

"It appears to be the same poison Iris had," said Faith. "We have to remove it."

"Help me!"

Falcon turned to the sight of a whimpering woman. In her hands she held an unconscious young girl. Her arms and legs dangled uselessly. Her lips and eyes were rimmed with darkness.

"My baby!" yelled the hysterical woman. "Something is wrong with her."

"Set her down here," ordered Faith, motioning to one of the empty beds.

The woman did as instructed.

Faith pulled out a clean knife from the bag and handed it to Father Lucien. "You know what to."

The healers went to work.

Falcon faced the woman. "What did your daughter have to drink or eat this morning?"

"Nothing to eat. All she had was a mug of water. But it couldn't have been that. That water was fresh."

As Faith and the father finished working on the boy, another woman came in clutching a girl in her arms.

Water? Falcon stood, lost in thought. That was the same thing the restaurant owner had told him. Which meant the man had been telling the truth.

"I'll be back," said Falcon.

"Where are you going?" asked Faith.

"To warn everyone about the water." As he headed for the city square, the same question raced through his head. If it wasn't the owner who had poisoned the villagers, who had?

~~~

It was midday when Falcon marched into the inn. Faith sat on a red sofa with her face dug into her hands.

"How are the children?" asked Falcon.

Faith looked up. "Better. They'll all be fine in a few days."

"That's good."

"I would feel better if we knew who did this. What are we going to do?"

"I'm afraid there is nothing we can do. We've done what we can by tending to the children and figuring out the source of the poison. But no, we must keep moving. The authorities from K'vitch will have to figure out who is behind this."

"I can't abandon them," said Faith. "They need my healing abilities."

Falcon rubbed his eyes, pondering what to do. He had to continue on with his mission. But, at the same time, he couldn't leave Faith behind. What if one of those psychos came looking for her?

All of a sudden, a guard rushed into the inn. "It happened again."

"What happened?" said Falcon. "Has someone else been poisoned?"

"No," said the guard, struggling to catch his breath. "Even worse."

Worse? What could possibly be worse than a poisoning?

Faith stood. "Is Iris in trouble?"

The guard lowered his gaze. "That's the thing. I don't know. All the children from the infirmary have disappeared."

CHAPTER 15

Falcon rushed into the empty infirmary, followed closely by Faith.

"I don't see her," said Faith, gasping for air.

Father Lucien sat silently on a dark chair, staring at the floor. "She was taken."

"Yes, we can see that," said Falcon, sighing in frustration. "Do you have any information that is actually helpful?"

Father Lucien nodded his head. "Still letting your emotions get the better of you, I see."

Falcon stared at the man, refusing to answer. This wasn't about him. It was about Iris.

"I was in my dormitory when I heard what sounded like a window panel sliding open. I made great haste and managed to catch the culprit sneaking out that window, carrying young Iris over his shoulder."

Falcon examined the window. "What about the other children? The kidnapper couldn't possibly have carried all four of them at once."

"Maybe it was done over multiple trips," said Faith. She examined the shattered glass. "But what use is there for kidnapping Iris? And why break the window after going to such lengths to keep quiet?"

"I have no idea." Falcon stared out the window. "But these tracks lead into the forest. My guess is that he wasn't counting on Father Lucien walking in on him."

The father stood from his chair. "What makes you think it's a he and not a she?"

"Just a hunch. There are not many women who could run out through a window with a body in tow."

"Maybe you're right," Father Lucien agreed. "Regardless. I'm sorry that I was unable to be of more assistance."

"I wouldn't be too sure about that." Falcon hurried outdoors, motioning for Faith and the father to follow. The moonlight illuminated a path of bent and cracked branches leading into the forest. "You seemed to have startled our friend enough to make him sloppy."

"And leave a path for us to follow," Faith added.

"But I'm afraid the moonlight is not nearly enough," said Father Lucien. "You won't be able to pick up the tracks until morning. By then Iris could be forever lost, or worse."

Faith put one hand to the sky. "Lihtan." In an instant, dozens of small dancing lights appeared in front of her. They converged, creating a fist-sized ball of bright light that illuminated the path before them.

The father stared in awe. "You are truly full of surprises."

Faith smiled and turned to Falcon. "After you?"

"Yes, let's move."

"Fortune be with you," said Father Lucien as Falcon and Faith moved into the thick forest.

"Thank you, sir," said Faith.

Falcon remained quiet. This culprit had made a big mistake. Falcon had grown fond of Iris in the short time he'd known her. When he found the kidnapper, he would make him regret ever laying his hands on her.

Deeper and deeper they went.

"Wait," said Faith.

Falcon stopped. "Why?"

Faith leaned down and picked up a piece of a broken branch. The ball of light glided above her, moving up and down as if floating on water. "These tracks aren't right."

Falcon stared at the path of footsteps leading to the East. "What's the problem? Let's continue on."

Faith scanned her surroundings. "There." She pointed toward the southwest.

Falcon stared at where Faith had pointed, but no matter how much he scrutinized, he couldn't figure out what he was supposed to be looking at. All he saw were the same dark trees and plants.

"The tracks leading to the East are too deliberate, almost as if someone wants us to follow them," said Faith.

"We don't have much of a choice. It's the only lead we have to follow."

"No." Her eyes remained fixed to the southwest. "You see these mooningdale plants?"

Falcon stared at the small insignificant green stems that burst from the forest floor. "Yes, what of them?"

"These plants naturally grow with a slight arch toward the East. But these flowers are all ramrod straight. Someone tampered with them."

Falcon took a look at the flowers, recalling that Faith had spent her entire childhood roaming the woods of Asturia.

"But Father Lucien only saw one person, not two. Who could have had the time to create a fake set of footprints?"

"Maybe it wasn't someone else."

Falcon narrowed his eyes. "What do you mean?"

Faith lowered her voice, as if someone might overhear their private conversation. "What if it was some type of wielding?"

"I never heard of any wielding that could do that."

"Exactly. It could be some type of dark wielding…or worse."

Falcon winced at the sudden ache in his chest. There was only one element that he knew worse than darkness. It was an element that raged within him—chaos.

"If I'm right," said Faith, "it could mean that the Suteckh are involved with all disappearances, or maybe even Volcseck."

"Then we have no time to waste," said Falcon with renewed vigor. "I can't wait to get my hands on that monster."

"Don't go too overboard," she said as she stepped over the flowers. She moved in zigzags without saying a word. Once in a while she would stop and pick up a slab of rock, or sniff a nearby plant. But then she would continue on at a determined pace.

"Are you sure we're going the right way?" he asked, wary of voicing his doubts. He had no desire to hurt her feelings. "I haven't seen any tracks in ages."

"I'm sure," she assured him. "It's not always what you see, Falcon. Sometimes it's what you don't see."

Falcon nodded as if he actually understood what she was talking about.

Finally, after what seemed like an eternity, they arrived at a small clearing.

"There's nothing here."

Faith moved forward to a trio of thick-leaved bushes. "Dorrington bushes don't naturally grow this close together. Someone planted them, almost as if they were trying to…" She grunted as she pushed the husky branches to the side, revealing an entrance to a dark cave. "Hide something."

"Great job," said Falcon, glad that he had decided to trust Faith.

She nodded. "I say we move in quietly from here on out. We don't want to alert whoever is in here that we stumbled onto their hideout."

"Yes," agreed Falcon, his admiration growing for the young holy wielder.

They crept through the thin cave, their only source of brightness coming from the light floating above them. Falcon made out the tan cave walls. There was writing on some of them, as if someone had taken a rock to them. He read the messages quietly.

He will be upon the world.

No one can stop him.

The deeper they moved into the cave, the more erratic the messages became. Even the writing itself grew increasingly abnormal, as if a crazed lunatic had etched it.

His stomach turned as he continued to read.

The tRue mastER awakens.

VolCsecK is but a PreTENDer.

ChAOs to the World.

Chaos CHAos CHAOS cHaos.

Judging by Faith's trembling lips, Falcon mused she was having the same thoughts as him. Was Shal-Volcseck somehow involved in this?

A sudden high-pitched voice forced Falcon back to reality.

"Whoever is speaking sounds close," whispered Faith. "It doesn't seem like they know we're here."

Falcon nodded and signaled Faith to keep following the voice. He was eager to get to the bottom of this mystery.

Seconds later, the tunnel came to an abrupt end. They stood in a massive opening. The high domed-shaped rock ceiling easily reached over thirty feet high. Crystal-clear water flowed through an opening in the ceiling and into the cave, falling gently into a pool of water.

Falcon ignored the scenery as his eyes settled on the dozens of human-sized crystals that lay side-by-side, creating a circle of gems. Inside each of the gems lay a child, including Iris. Each child had their eyes closed and their hands by their side.

"Those poor children," said Faith, concern in her voice. "Do you think they're still alive?"

"I hope so," answered Falcon as he noticed a cloaked figure at the center of the room, chanting in a raspy masculine voice. At first his voice was barely audible, but with each passing second it grew in volume until it became a shout.

"Do you understand anything he's saying?" asked Falcon.

"No, but it sounds a lot like a summoning chant, doesn't it?"

Falcon's eyes widened as he realized Faith was right. Only advanced element summoning used ancient languages.

He had to act quickly before the summoning could be finished. Without much of a plan, he hopped down to the hard floor, landing with a loud thump.

From within the veil, Lakirk's brow rose in recognition.

Falcon stumbled back. "What are you doing here?"

The mayor's son flashed a grin. "Oh, it's you. I knew you coming to K'vitch would prove troublesome."

"Lakirk? But why?" stuttered Faith as she landed behind Falcon. "These are the children of the village. The same village your father is mayor of."

Lakirk tossed the cloak aside, revealing a patch of untamed hair. His eyes darted back and forth between Falcon and Faith as he licked his lips. "Please. That failure is no father of mine."

"His mind is broken," said Falcon. "Who knows what kind of dark arts he's been dwelling in."

Lakirk cackled loudly as he clutched his stomach. "Oh no, not darkness. I serve something far greater."

"Greater?" echoed Falcon, taking a step forward. Perhaps he could slowly close the distance between them and put an end to this madness.

Lakirk held up his index finger and moved it side to side. "Stay back, Rohad. If you make another move, I'll cut these roots and you can say goodbye to the poor children, including your little friend."

Falcon froze, noticing the blue tubes permeating from each of the crystals. The blue lines all led to a dark corner of the cave. "Where do those roots go to? What are you hiding?"

"I sense life-energy inside those tubes," said Faith. "You're sucking it from the children, aren't you?"

Lakirk's eye's twitched. "Clever little girl." He turned to Falcon as he scratched his flaky skin. "Much smarter than this brute friend of yours. But it makes no difference. In a minute he'll be back, and everyone in Va'siel will be no more."

Falcon thought back to the injured Volcseck. Could it be that Lakirk was using the children's life force to heal that monster?

Lakirk's hands trembled as he reached for the air. "Yes. Yes. Back. Back. Back. The true master back."

"I knew it," said Falcon. "You're aiding Shal-Volcseck."

Lakirk's hands shot down. "You truly are an idiot, aren't you? I serve the true lord of chaos, not that cheap imitation you call Volcseck."

True lord of chaos?

"I can tell by that look on your face that you're still confused." Lakirk tilted his jittery head to the side. "And people say I'm stupid."

"Stop with the riddles and get to the point," Falcon ordered, anger boiling within him. "There is only one chaos wielder in Va'siel, everyone knows that."

"That's what I thought too." He held up his head in grandiose fashion as he paced between the crystals. "But then his voice came to me one night. He awoke me from my ignorance and gave my insignificant life a purpose."

"And what was that?" asked Faith. "To kidnap children and kill them?"

"More or less. The energy of children is the purest there is, and it's also the easiest to control. That makes it ideal for my father to return from his long slumber."

"You're just a pawn," said Falcon, taking another step forward. That was the third step he had taken without Lakirk noticing. If he could just keep him talking, then perhaps he still had a chance to close the gap and save the children. "It was Volcseck who created those fake tracks. He's been aiding you from the shadows."

Lakirk banged one of the crystals with his fist. "No!" He grabbed a chunk of his hair and pulled it off his scalp as he gritted his teeth.

Falcon took another step.

"Haven't you been listening? I am a servant, but not of Shal-Volcseck. I serve…" For once Lakirk held still as he gazed at Falcon and Faith. The shadows of the cave darkened half of his face, giving him an eerie appearance. "Shal-Demetrius."

"Shal-Demetrius?" Falcon grimaced. "Now I know you're a lunatic."

171

"He might be crazy," Faith suggested, "but there might be some truth to what he says. I sense an extremely strong essence of chaos coming from that corner of the cave."

Falcon's mouth went dry as his worries returned. "It must be Volcseck."

"No!" yelled Lakirk, laughing hysterically. "It was Lord Demetrius who trained that imposter you call Volcseck. It was Demetrius who took him under his wing and taught him everything he knows. But then that imposter betrayed him and…and…and…." He took a deep breath. "It makes no difference. The true lord's ascension to power is at hand. And once he returns, he will destroy all. Volcseck will be the first to feel his wrath, followed by every living being in Va'siel."

The knot in Falcon's stomach tightened. One chaos wielder was bad enough. Could it be possible that there was really another lord of chaos? Not wanting to find out, he willed himself forward.

Lakirk, too engrossed with his speech, didn't seem to notice as Falcon closed the distance between them. By the time the servant of chaos noticed Falcon's movement, the void wielder was directly beside him.

But instead of panicking, like Falcon had expected, Lakirk grinned as he waved goodbye.

Falcon's hand cut air as the crazed man teleported out of the way.

"A chaos wielder must be helping him," said Faith.

172

Though Lakirk was gone, his voice echoed through the cave. "It's too late, idiot. He comes. He comes. He comes. He comes."

A sharp crack burst from the dark corner where the roots gathered.

"Lihtan." Faith's ball of light took to the air, illuminating every corner of the cave.

Falcon finally got a clear view of his entire surroundings, including the dark corner, where a human-shaped shadow pushed itself out of a vertical crystal.

Glass shattered on the floor, and the aroma of blood assaulted Falcon's senses.

"W…what is that?" stuttered Faith.

Falcon remained quiet, unsure of what to say.

A dark, hunched figure stumbled forward, with its head facing to the floor. Long hair flowed down its back. The mysterious being wore what appeared to be a beggar's tunic, along with a set of ragged pants.

Falcon stumbled back as his eyes settled on the black emblem with red cracks. "Impossible. That's a chaos emblem."

"I'm free." The chaos wielder's loud cackle bounced off the cave walls. "The end is finally here."

CHAPTER 16

A hard tap on the shoulder snapped Aya awake. "How ya sleep, princess?" asked Rika, standing over Aya.

Aya picked herself up off the floor. "Fine, thanks." She had not gotten much rest. Thoughts of Selene made sleep impossible, but she was not about to tell that to anyone.

Rika tossed a bowl at her.

Aya caught it, eyeing the white gunk inside the bowl suspiciously. "What is this?"

Rika rolled her eyes. "Why, food, of course. What else?" She stomped away, muttering to herself. Aya only managed to hear the words "useless" and "pathetic."

"Morning," said Sheridan, stuffing a spoonful of food into his mouth. He held a bowl in his hands. "This oatmeal is great, isn't it? They put in some type of syrup that only grows on these trees. Maybe they'll give me the recipe."

"Um, yeah." Aya took a look around the camp. Rika was strapping a bow and quiver to her back. By a brown tent stood Keira with her three bears, deep in conversation. She made grandiose movements with her hands, and Aya wondered if the bears could actually understand what their master was telling them. At Keira's waist hung a long katana with a jeweled handle.

"What's going on?" Aya asked. "Are we going into battle?"

"Don't know," said Sheridan. "I asked, but no one will tell me anything. I don't care though. I'd much rather ask where I can get another serving of this oatmeal."

Aya handed him her bowl. "Here, take mine."

Sheridan hopped in place. "Thanks!"

"Don't worry about it." She headed over to Raji, who stood silently by the end of the camp. "What's going on here?"

Raji crossed his arms, eyeing her from top to bottom.

"Hey, I asked you a question."

"Raji has a job to do. There is no knowing when someone may attack," interrupted Keira, walking toward her. "What do you need?"

"I won't be much help without information."

"You won't be any help with or without information," said Keira.

Aya ignored the comment. "I need to know what is going on."

"If you must know, we are readying for an attack on an outpost Hotaru has west of here."

"Why west? Isn't Sugiko east of here?"

Keira sighed impatiently. "Don't worry about the details. You stick to staying out of my way. Let me figure out strategy. Got it?"

175

"Keira?" interrupted Nanake, appearing out of nowhere. "Our guest needs to know the plan if she is to aid us."

"No," Keira shot back. "Why would I tell this Rohad our strategy? So she can divulge our plans to Hotaru? I don't think so."

Aya narrowed her gaze. "I would never do that. I'm loyal to your cause."

"Please." Keira took a step toward Aya. "When my uncle makes you a better offer, we'll see where your loyalty lies. All Rohads are the same. Just a lot of traitorous scum."

Nanake stomped her cane on the ground. "Keira. That's enough!"

"Whatever." She waved her hand dismissively as she stomped away.

"Please, forgive her," begged Nanake.

"It's fine," said Aya, wondering where so much hate stemmed from. "Could you please tell me what's going on?"

"Of course. We are launching an attack on the outpost west of here. Hotaru has four outposts around Sugiko, one to the west, east, south, and north. Each outpost has enough weapons, armored suits, emblems, and, more importantly, food to last us months."

"Great plan," said Sheridan, sneaking behind Aya. "We'll go from outpost to outpost, taking all their materials. Once we have them, we'll launch our attack and take back Sugiko."

Aya grimaced, not fully convinced of the logic behind the plan. "Wouldn't attacking each of the outposts just wear down morale? You may be able to take the first one or two, but Hotaru will only strengthen his last outposts, which will not only make an attack on them highly predictable and nearly impossible to take over." She took a breath. "And even if you do manage to take them over, you have not won much. You'll still be no closer to having Sugiko back, and you will have lost so many lives in the process that an attack on the city will prove fruitless."

Nanake nodded. "The attack on the west outpost is only a diversion. If we take it over, Hotaru will surely send more men to his other three outposts, expecting an attack on them. This will in turn weaken the defense of the city."

"And make an attack on Sugiko a surprise attack," added Aya, finally understanding the situation. "Since Hotaru will be expecting an attack on his outposts, not the capital city."

Nanake stared at Aya and offered a smile. "You have a great mind for strategy. I'm glad you Rohads are here to aid us."

"Your people came up with a sound strategy all by yourselves. I'm sure you would have done fine by yourselves."

"Actually, the entire plan was conceived by my granddaughter. Everyone else wanted to storm the castle. You and she are more alike than she cares to admit."

177

Aya played with her fingers, unsure of what to say. She wasn't exactly fond of being compared to Keira. The girl had some serious anger problems.

"Well, I feel stupid," said Sheridan, breaking the awkward silence. "I guess I'm not a genius like you ladies."

"I'm sure you have your virtues," said Nanake in a reassuring voice.

"Like eating!" yelled Sheridan, rushing toward the cook who had just announced that there were extra plates of oatmeal available.

"Excuse me," said Aya. "I better get ready. Thank you for your trust."

The elder woman patted Aya on the shoulder. "Of course. Be safe, young lady."

Aya made her way back to her sleeping bag to gather her weapons. From the edge of her view, she noticed Keira eyeing her with rage. She probably wasn't fond of having her grandmother taking a liking to her.

Too bad, thought Aya, as she strapped her baton sticks to her waist.

"We have a long march through the forest, men," said Keira. "It's going to be a hot day, so drink plenty of water. Raji and I will lead the group." The young princess raised her hands. "Are you ready to reclaim our home?"

A thunderous chorus of "Yes!" was her answer.

"Good!" responded Keira.

Nanake trudged over to Rika and gave her a hug. She then embraced Keira as well.

"I'll be careful, grandma," Aya overheard Keira say. "I'm sorry for the way I spoke to you earlier."

"Think nothing of it. Just promise me you'll be safe. I love you with all my heart."

For the first time since she'd met her, the princess's features softened ever so slightly. "I love you too." Her face stiffened as she moved in front of her men. Her three bears followed behind her. "Let's move."

The loud sound of hundreds of marching boots radiated through the air, drowning out the chirping of the birds.

They walked for hours.

Sheridan wiped his forehead in exhaustion. "This humid weather is killing me."

Aya ran her fingers past a smooth vine. She felt for the familiar fussy end, then she snapped it in half and tossed it to her companion. "Squeeze the end, it has fresh water."

Water poured out of Sheridan's mouth as he pushed the vine with both hands. "Thank you, Nakatomi. That's why I love coming on missions with you. You have knowledge of the most useless things imaginable."

Aya brought her finger to her lips. "Shhh… Don't talk so much. It's a waste of energy."

"Nakatomi. I have plenty of energy. In fact there was this one time that I…"

179

Aya drowned out Sheridan as she gazed at the princess before her. She walked with such determination that it was hard to believe she was blind. She moved over logs, under branches, and around puddles with ease. Never once did she stray from the path that cut a zigzag through the trees. Her head never moved. It remained ramrod straight.

The bears, on the other hand, constantly moved their heads left, right, up, and down. Aya could only assume they did this so their master wouldn't miss anything.

"Stop," ordered Keira, after an arduous morning of marching. They stood next to a steep cliff. A variety of green-leaved trees surrounded them. "We're near the outpost. Raji and I will lead the charge. Everyone else will follow behind. I want our ten archers to stay back and lend aid from a distance. No rushing in for close combat." Keira turned to the face-painted girl beside her. "I'm talking to you, Rika."

"I get it," answered the little girl. "I won't make the same mistake as last—"

It all happened in a split second. One moment only the voice of Rika could be heard, the next the thunderous battle cry of men filled the air as Hotaru's soldiers spilled out of the bushes.

Two black and red uniformed men went straight at Aya with katana in hand. She hopped back while simultaneously taking hold of the first soldier's sword and running it through his counterpart. She delivered a side hand attack to the second assailant's neck. The man crumpled down.

At her side, Raji downed three enemies with a single punch. A masked soldier dashed behind the gigantic warrior and forced a spear through Raji's leg. Without flinching or making a sound, Raji picked his attacker up by the neck and tossed the screaming soldier down the cliff. He pulled the spear out of his body and threw it. The spear cut down a screaming man who stood on a tree branch, shooting arrows.

A faint moan caught Aya's attention. At the edge of the cliff stood a trembling Rika. Two soldiers moved toward her.

Aya dashed toward them.

Before she could reach Rika, a swift blur knocked the first soldier down. It took a second for Aya to realize that it was Keira. The princess executed a vicious kick to the man's ribs. He went down as the sound of bones cracking drowned out all other noise.

A second later, the brown bear took hold of the second soldier. Aya looked away as the animal's fangs dug into the man's neck, turning a pained wail into a gargle of noises.

"Good job," said Sheridan, patting the bear on the back. "It looks like that was the last of them."

"Leave my bear alone," snapped Keira. "Unless you want to be next."

Sheridan held up his hands in a defensive position, though his smile remained.

"H-how c…could…" Rika took a breath. "How could they have known we were coming?"

"They didn't," said Keira. "Those were a small group of scouts who patrol the area. Pretty stupid of 'em to attack a hundred of us with such a small force."

Rika remained shaking. "How could ya know? Maybe someone betrayed us."

Aya met her gaze. "Scout groups only operate in groups of a dozen. And there were twelve soldiers here." As soon as the words left her mouth she realized that something was amiss. The bears were moving from side to side, which meant Keira must have come to the same conclusion.

There were three dead men besides Raji. Two other soldiers lay by the cliff. Aya herself had downed two soldiers. Three other soldiers' corpses were spread out through the skirmish area. That only made ten soldiers. Even if she added the one soldier who was tossed down to his demise, there was still one missing.

"There's one of 'em missing," said Keira, a second before Aya made the same announcement. "There!"

Raji punched the tree that Keira had pointed at, causing it to tremble ferociously. From atop the bushes a grunting soldier fell, along with dozens of leaves.

The words "Earth fall" rang in Aya's ear.

Rika froze in place as the ground under her collapsed.

Keira dashed forward and shoved her cousin out of the way, but now she stood on the crumbling earth.

Aya ran and threw herself on the ground. She caught Keira's hand just as she plummeted down. The white bear also extended his arm.

The ground under them shattered in a thousand places.

The white bear roared.

Keira cursed.

Aya screamed.

The three of them plummeted to the darkness below.

CHAPTER 17

Falcon winced as the newcomer tilted his head up, revealing an uncountable series of deep wrinkles. Half of his face remained obscured in darkness; though his crooked teeth remained visible as he smiled.

This can't be happening. It's bad enough Va'siel has to deal with one chaos wielder. Now two… No, I have to put a stop to this here and now.

Falcon readied his katana and rushed forward. The chaos wielder's dirt-caked tunic received a small slice as the sword cut through it.

Shal-Demetrius, however, remained in one piece as he hopped back.

Falcon followed with a series of sword strikes as the chaos wielder continued his retreat. He grinned as the old man's back reached the wall. He'd been caught off-guard by the ancient man's quick movement, but now there was no way to escape. "It's over." He swiped his katana in a downward motion.

With a smile on his face, Demetrius dodged to the side. The sword ricocheted against the wall. "Good form, young warrior. But too reckless."

Falcon grunted and dove for another attack.

"Almost had me there," mocked Demetrius. "Precision is overrated. Keep throwing wild attacks. I'm sure one day an attack will find its mark."

"Who needs precision when you got power?" said Falcon, ignoring Demetrius's sarcasm. Falcon took a step back. He needed space for this next attack. "Let's see you dodge this." A web of yellow coursed through his emblem as he created a wall of lightning. The air cracked loudly as it moved forward as one.

Demetrius's emblem glowed a crimson red as he inhaled deeply. "Ingest."

Falcon rubbed his brow in disbelief as the lightning flowed into the old man's mouth. A loud burp followed.

"That was delicious." Demetrius licked his dry lips. "So you're a lightning wielder, I see. Thank you for the meal."

"By the elements," said Falcon, still in disbelief. "How did—" It doesn't matter how. It's just some more of that evil chaos. The important thing is to finish this.

"Falcon," said Faith from behind Falcon. "Stop."

"Don't worry," said Falcon. "I plan to put a stop to this."

Demetrius yawned as he ran his skeletal hands through his untamed hair. "It's going to take more than simple lightning to bring down a chaos wielder."

"I got more for you, fiend."

Demetrius responded with an amused, "Oh."

185

A soft tap landed on Falcon's shoulder. "Don't you worry, Faith," he assured her before she could speak. "I got this under control. If he wants to eat energy, I'll give him some that will end him." He hoped he sounded more confident than he felt. He'd been putting a lot of training into poison wielding, with erratic results. Would it be enough? "Gas of Garrados!" He spread his legs just like he had seen in the tutorial manuscripts. It seemed to be working, because a faint blue mist formed at his fingertips.

Just when Falcon thought he had the hang of it, the mist dissolved without so much as a whimper, causing a wave of rage to spread through him. How can I be this weak?

A sudden loud snap rang in Falcon's ears. A second later an explosion burst from the ground, sending him flying into a wall.

The smell of fresh fire filled Falcon's nostrils as he got back to his feet. The hit had dazed him a bit, but he was fine.

Demetrius seemed, for the first time, to waver. "How did you chaos wield?"

"Don't you worry about that," said Falcon, trying to keep the shakiness in his voice in check. He stared down at his emblem and his heart nearly stopped. Sure enough it had dark red cracks on it. I chaos wielded. I'm a monster.

"I asked you a question, boy. Answer me!"

Falcon shook himself back to the present. He picked up his katana from the floor. His chest ached as he took a step toward his enemy. No matter how much he wanted to concentrate on Demetrius, he couldn't get over the fact that he was no different than Volcseck.

Then, without warning, the pain in his chest dissolved as warm hands touched his shoulders. His trembling body returned to normal and his mind relaxed.

"Is that better?" breathed a honeyed voice in his ear.

"Faith?"

"Yes, it's me. Calm down."

"I-I-I," he was at peace, but confused. "What are you doing? This is not the time for this. We m…must stop." He stumbled forward. Faith pulled him back before he crashed to the ground. "Shal-Demetrius is—"

"Not the enemy," finished Faith. "He hasn't attacked you once this entire time. All his moves have been purely defensive."

His confused mind returned to normal as Faith removed her hands. A hint of rage also returned, though not as strong as before. "Of course he's the enemy."

Faith walked by Falcon and extended her hand to the chaos wielder. "Hello, sir. I'm Faith Hemstath. Pleasure to meet you."

Demetrius brought his hand up, and Falcon took a step forward in response. Faith was obviously under some kind of chaos trance and he didn't plan to stand idly by as the old man attacked her.

But to his surprise, Demetrius didn't produce a weapon or even try to wield as Falcon had expected. Instead he held his hand directly in front of Faith's and stared in apparent amusement.

"Why are you showing me your hand?" asked Demetrius.

She took his hand and shook it. "It's called a handshake. It's a way to say hello."

Demetrius scratched his head. "What a strange way to say hello. In my day a simple declaration of one's clan served as introduction. I suppose a lot changes in ten thousand years."

"You were in that crystal for ten thousand years?" exclaimed Falcon.

"Technically it's sap, not a crystal. And yes, I was there for that long. Give or take a few centuries." The old man spoke in a casual voice, as if being trapped for so long was an everyday occurrence.

Falcon turned back to Faith, hoping for an explanation. "But h…how?"

"How about we focus on getting these poor children free," said Demetrius, "instead of focusing on me."

"Yes," added Faith. "We should hurry before they're fully drained."

"Not to worry. When I was inside the chaos sap I was vaguely aware of what was going on. I managed to suppress the energy being drained into my body enough so that none of the children were in any mortal danger. All you have to do now is release them."

"Me?" asked Faith, her voice filled with shock.

"Yes," said Demetrius, moving beside Faith. Falcon readied himself; he didn't fully trust the newcomer. "You're a holy wielder, are you not?"

Faith held up her hand, showcasing her pristine emblem. "Yes."

"And I imagine you're the only holy wielder in Va'siel."

"I'm the only one I know of."

Demetrius nodded. "Then that means you have never had any proper holy training." He brought his hand to his wrinkled chin as if deep in thought. A second later he took an unexpected jump four feet in the air, much higher than Falcon ever expected such an ancient person to jump to. "No matter. From what I just saw, your holy wielding is enough to suppress the chaos."

"Suppress?" asked Falcon. He could tell that Faith was just as confused as him.

"Every element has a natural counter. Fire and water. Earth and lightning." He pointed at Faith. "Holy is a natural counter to both darkness and chaos. I would have thought that, in ten thousand years, youth would have grown wiser. I suppose not."

"So what do I do?" asked Faith, obviously not as annoyed by the old man's words as Falcon was.

"Do the same thing that you did for your thick-headed friend here a minute ago to calm him down."

Faith slowly moved forward and placed her hand on the sap crystal that contained Iris. A radiant yellow light traveled from her hands and into the crystal. A second later the sap dissolved, creating a pile of clear yellowish goo on the cave floor.

A gargled cough was the first noise Iris made, followed by a series of moans. Suddenly she sat upward, breathing quickly. "W-w-where am I? Let me go, Lakirk. Let me go! Y-you won't…"

"Relax, Iris. You're safe now."

"That's right, you are," added Falcon, keeping a watchful eye on Demetrius.

Iris's words tumbled over each other. "The last thing I remember was Lakirk. He took me. T…tried to…"

"Everything is fine now." Faith put her arms around the small girl. "You're going to be fine."

Iris dug her head into Faith's jacket as she sobbed. When she finally stopped a minute later, Faith quickly freed the remaining children. It took a moment for them to adjust back to reality, but they were all breathing and moving normally.

"So what is it that you want?" Falcon asked, facing Demetrius. "Why did you influence Lakirk into freeing you?"

"Me?" He pointed a long finger at himself. "I want nothing more than to rest. Lakirk acted of his own accord."

"Sure he did," said Falcon. "How convenient that you're now free. No one benefited more from this than you. You are responsible, chaos wielder. Who else could it have been?"

"Sure, blame the chaos wielder," said Demetrius, his voice filled with sarcasm. "Has it ever occurred to you that not all chaos wielders are bad?"

Falcon remained silent. He had indeed never thought of chaos wielders as anything but pure evil.

"Besides," Demetrius added, "you're a chaos wielder yourself."

"I'm no chaos wielder!" snapped Falcon.

Demetrius chuckled. "Bold words for someone who just chaos wielded, and quite badly, I might add. You have no control."

Falcon grimaced. He'd spent his entire life hearing how he had no control. The last thing he needed was to hear it from a chaos wielder.

"But that can be remedied," continued Demetrius. "I can show you how to control it, instead of having it control you."

"You can't be serious. Why would I want to be taught by you?"

"Because you have no one else who can teach you. And it's painfully obvious you need the tutelage. Tell me, have you ever lost control? Allowed your inner rage take over you?"

The words of the ancient man echoed in Falcon's head as he recalled the time at the arena when he'd turned into a monster. He had been so engrossed that he had almost attacked Aya. Perhaps Demetrius's offer was worth considering.

"Yes, Falcon," cheered Iris, apparently back to her old self. "Become more powerful so you can catch Lakirk and kick his behind."

Falcon turned to Faith, realizing that if he truly wanted to protect her and Aya, he needed to push his wants aside and takes Demetrius's offer. "I accept your offer, but only for a few days. I have other things to attend to."

Demetrius took a breath, and Falcon wondered why the old man wanted to teach him in the first place. "Good!" He pumped his fists and did a little dance that involved hip-hopping round on one leg. "You're about to be trained by the most powerful, cunning, and let's not forget amazing wielder of all the land." He cleared his throat. "The legendary chaos wielder, Shal-Demetrius."

Faith clapped.

Iris and the kids giggled.

Falcon stood at a loss for words at the strange antics. His palm struck his forehead as he wondered what in the world he had gotten himself into.

CHAPTER 18

Aya rubbed her eyes. Slowly, the green blur in front of her turned into large leaves hanging from thick long trees.

A second later two heads appeared looking down on her. One belonged to a girl; the other one was a large, white, furred mess.

"Took you long enough," said Keira, rolling her eyes. She patted her bear. "What do you think, Loriko? How long do you think she'll survive before she dies?"

Loriko grunted and moved behind Keira.

The blind girl laughed. "You're right."

"How did we survive that fall?" asked Aya, picking herself up. She stared up. A thick gray mist that flowed miles above her made it impossible to see the top of the cliff.

"Loriko, of course," said Keira knowingly. "My bears have all been trained to survive…uncommon situations. Loriko here, for example, pulled us in while we were falling, then took most of the brunt of the blows as we slammed into the trees. Sure, slowing down by willingly crashing into branches is not the best of options, but it beats breaking your fall with your face."

"I don't think we chose to crash into the branches. We just did. It's not like we had much of a choice in the matter."

"That's where you're wrong. Loriko eyed the thickest branches as we fell and made sure to land on those. All while holding onto us while falling on her back." There was an undistinguishable hint of pride in Keira's voice.

"That sounds so far-fetched that—" Aya winced as she noticed the scratches on Loriko's back. Does it really matter? Were alive, and that's all that matters. "Thank you, Loriko."

Keira grimaced. "Lie down." The bear did as instructed. Keira then reached in her pocket and pulled out a ball of wrapped leaves. She opened them, revealing a glittering powder.

"What's that?"

Without answering, the blind girl cautiously put her hand on her bear's back and ran her hands through the fur.

Why is she moving so slow? And that's when it hit her. Since Keira was so far from her other bears, she was cut off from their sight. She only had Loriko to rely on.

"Let me do that," said Aya, reaching for the shiny medicine.

"No! You don't know where to put the medicine. I do."

Aya stepped back. "Sorry."

The bear growled loudly as Keira applied a dash of the powder inside the cut. But it remained a place.

"That's amazing," said Aya. "How did you ever gain such obedience from an animal?"

Keira rolled her cloudy eyes. "It's not obedience. It's loyalty, a loyalty that is created between two friends. It is something that a Rohad could never understand."

"That's not true. I know plenty of loyal Rohads." Something inside of her twisted in annoyance.

"Sure, tell that to my parents who…" She waved her hand. "Forget about it. Why bother explaining to someone like you?" Keira put the remaining medicine in her pocket. "And just so we're clear: I know you tried to save me because you're expecting some kind of reward. Well, I'm sorry to disappoint you, but you're not getting more than whatever the contract says. Got it?"

Aya took a calming breath, opting to forego future discussion. "Sure. Now how about we concentrate on the issue at hand. How are going to get back up the cliff? This way up appears to be littered with loose rocks. We won't make it if we try to climb it."

"Climb it?" asked Keira, shaking her head slightly. "Why would we do that?"

"How else are we supposed to get back to the others?"

Keira slammed the palm of her hand on her head. "We're not going back to the group. We're going to continue on the mission."

"But you're their leader. You have to be there to guide them."

"Exactly. And I will be there. Raji will lead them to the spot where we're supposed to meet. We just have to make sure we're there too."

"I'm not sure that's a sound plan," said Aya, weighing her options. "We don't know if they'll even be there. Since you fell they may organize a search party instead of moving toward the rendezvous point. I think we should—"

"Too bad what you think doesn't matter. I'm the paying client and you do as I say, is that clear?"

Aya steadied herself. "Of course, let's go."

And without saying another word, with her guide beside her, Keira took off into the thick shrubbery. Aya followed close behind. Seconds later Aya ducked as a thick branch almost smacked her across the face.

"Careful there," said Keira with a snicker. Every few seconds Keira would "accidentally" let loose a branch toward Aya followed by "Sorry, did I hit you, mercenary?" or "Watch your face."

But after moments of doing this and getting no response from Aya, Keira stopped talking and simply walked silently behind Loriko.

"We're going to need to get food soon," said Keira.

Aya pointed up at the trees. "There's plenty of fruit up there. I'll go get some down for us."

"What? You think I can't do it because I'm blind?"

"I didn't say that."

"I can climb a tree faster than you ever could. Just you see." She took off in a sprint and hopped on the tree trunk. From the ground, Loriko looked up, providing Keira with the sight she needed.

Aya picked up her speed and ran up the tree trunk, using the momentum to propel herself to the nearest branch. She then flipped to the branch above that. She kept on doing that, flipping and hopping from branch to branch. From the corner of her eye she noticed Keira was moving up the opposite tree at the same breakneck speed as her. How is she doing that without full visibility?

"Got it," said Keira. She stood on a thick branch. In her hands she held a bushel of circular fruits with a hairy exterior. "I knew that I was the fastest one here." She held tight to her fruits as she hopped down from branch to branch.

Aya pulled free a few hard purple fruits that dangled from the tree she had climbed. Once she felt like she had secured most of them in one hand, she moved down to the ground. She landed beside the princess.

"About time you got back," said Keira. She was taking large bites out of the fruit, which she had already peeled. "I hope you're not too sore that I beat you."

"It's fine." Aya studied the hard fruit in her hands. There didn't appear to be any way to peel it. That meant that she needed to break it open. She grabbed a nearby rock and hit the fruit a few times. The purple shell broke in pieces. Her stomach growled as she pulled the pieces off and revealed a fragrant soft center. Seeing the lump of chewy fruit reminded her how hungry she really was. She licked her lips and brought the fruit to her mouth.

Loriko danced around Keira in a fit of panic. He waved his paws around and grunted something, though Aya couldn't understand what he was trying to say.

Keira rolled her eyes. "Fine, you win. I'll tell her."

Loriko lay back down beside the princess.

Keira turned her gaze at Aya. "I wouldn't do that if I were you."

Aya paused, the fruit inches from her mouth. "Do what?"

"Do you even know what you're holding?"

"Yes. It's a mangosteen. Learning the different fruits and vegetables of Va'siel is required of all Rohads. Did you honestly think that I would just go around eating random foods I knew nothing about?"

"Well, those texts of yours missed something. That's not a mangosteen."

Aya cautiously moved the fruit back and studied it. It had the soft, white texture that the books at the Rohad library had described. She brought the fruit to her nose. The sweet aroma engulfed her nostrils, just as the books had said. She then studied the shell that had fallen on the floor. It was the way it was supposed to be, purple and hard. No matter how much she tried, she saw nothing out of the ordinary. Could it be that Keira was just toying with her? She certainly wouldn't put it past her.

"I think I see a vein popping out of that forehead of yours from all the thinking you're doing," said Keira in between bites. "Figure it out yet?"

"No, as far as I can tell there is nothing wrong with this fruit."

Keira grabbed the white fruit and pointed at it. "See those small pores?"

Aya made out small, barely visible dots at the bottom of the fruit.

"A real mangosteen doesn't have those," continued Keira. "What you're holding there is a larys fruit, which is safely edible once it's been cooked for at least a day. But if you eat it in its natural state, it will give you hallucinations for hours. Could be two hours or thirty. No one really knows how long. Either way, it's not something very pleasant."

Aya dropped the remaining larys fruits to the ground, feeling like a fool. How could she have been this stupid?

"Here." Keira tossed her one of her fruits. "It's the last rambutan, and I'm full. You eat it."

Aya quietly peeled off the hairy skin and ate the white insides. "Thanks for telling me before I ate it."

"Don't thank me. I would have let you eat it. Loriko here was the one complaining." She patted her bear. "Which reminds me. We have to get some food for Loriko. Bears don't eat fruit. And if Loriko doesn't stay properly fed, my vision link begins to dissipate. It's bad enough I lost my other eyes. I can't afford to lose Loriko's too."

Aya shoved her feeling of uselessness aside. She wished she had her bow with her so she could hunt. "Yes, of course. What did you have in mind?"

"Amazing!" came an excited shriek.

Aya turned in shock. In front of her stood a boy. He couldn't have been more than six years old. He had unruly dark hair and thick eyebrows. His bland clothes were ragged.

"Who are you and what are you doing here?" asked Keira. She seemed even more surprised than Aya.

"I'm Yuto. Well my real name is Yutomi Nagano Loa Gao of Nelia Port."

"Yes, yes. We get it. Your name is long. But what are you doing here?"

"Well that's a long story. At first my mom was like, 'Yuto, fetch some meat from the slaughterhouse.' And I said, 'But why me? Have Nari do it.' Nari is my little sister and she's as lazy as they come. Just the other day she had to fetch the eggs and she didn't do it. Her excuse was that she couldn't because the chicken was her best friend—"

"Get to the point, boy," snapped Keira. For once, Aya agreed with her.

"Of course. I was heading to the slaughterhouse when I heard some commotion. I got closer to see what it as and saw this bear of yours, oh yes. I did see it. I have never seen one up close. Well, I did once in the books Dad found in the gutter, but this is the first time I've seen one in real life."

"Your home is near?" asked Keira, her voice dripping with interest. "And if I heard you correctly, you said something about meat?"

"Keira," said Aya. "We can't take this poor family's food. It looks like they barely have enough."

"No," said Yuto. "We have a lot to go around. Father made a good catch the other day, oh yes he did. He said, 'Son, I'm the best hunter in Va'siel.' I never believed him, of course, because I know the best hunters are the Rohads."

Keira frowned.

"But that still didn't stop him from catching two full-grown male deer the other day," continued Yuto. "I say it's more luck than anything else. But now we have more food than anyone in Va'siel, oh yes we do."

Keira's frown turned into a smile. "You heard the boy. They have too much food, and we have a bear that needs food. It's perfect."

Aya scratched her head. Something didn't feel right. "I don't know. I think—"

"What you think doesn't matter. I'm the boss, remember?"

202

"It's settled then," said Yuto. "Follow me, I know the way, oh yes I do." He continued to ramble on as he led them through a path hidden behind a curtain of leaves. They ended at a small cabin surrounded by nature.

"Where have you been, Yuto?" said a short lady who tended to a slab of meat that rested above a fire. She paused when she saw that Yuto was not alone.

"I found these people out in the wilderness, oh yes I did. They need meat. I told them we have more than enough."

"I hope that we're not bothering you," said Aya.

The lady's color left her when she noticed the bear, but a second later it returned. "No. It's no bother. We have more than enough food. Please sit." She motioned toward a log that lay sprawled across the grass. "Yuto, go fetch your father. Tell them we have guests."

"Yes, Mom."

Yuto took off into the cabin.

Aya eyed the giant piece of meat that was roasting over the fire. Her stomach growled in hungry anticipation as the aroma of the salted meat passed by her. Loriko took to licking the air, as if he could taste the smell.

"My name is Nishi," said the woman. "Are you refugees?"

"No," said Keira.

Nishi turned the meat over. "We've had so many people pass through here lately, escaping the tyranny of Hotaru. Naturally, I assumed you were some of them."

"That's them, Father," said Yuto as he arrived with a skinny man beside him. "They're hungry, yes they are." The boy turned to a small girl who ran behind him. "See, Nari? I told you they had a white bear."

"Wow!" exclaimed the blue-eyed girl. She ran up to Loriko, but then seemed to think twice of it and staggered back. Aya suspected the bear's sharp fangs had something to do with her change of heart.

"You can touch Loriko if you want," said Keira, motioning for the kids to get closer.

The girl twirled her long ponytails. "But what if it bites me?"

Keira laughed. "Loriko doesn't attack anyone without my order. Go ahead."

"I'll do it," said Yuto. He slowly made his way to Loriko and ran his hands across the bear's back. Loriko growled so softly, it was as if he was purring.

"See?" said Keira. "Loriko likes being pampered."

This seemed to energize Nari with courage. She ran over to Loriko and touched his back.

The man smiled. "I'm Isamu. You honor us with your presence." He extended his hand.

Aya returned the smile and shook the man's hand. The sweat from his hands passed over to hers. As he moved over to Keira, Aya couldn't help to notice that his smile seemed forced.

"Are you passing by on a pilgrimage?" asked Nishi as she handed Aya a bowl of meat. "Kids, get off that poor creature!"

"Do we have to?" whined the children.

"Yes. Have some manners."

Both kids glumly got off the bear. Loriko seemed saddened too, until Nishi set an entire moose leg before him. He looked over at Keira, as if asking for permission. Once the blind girl gave him a nod, Loriko sank his teeth into the meat.

"Thanks for the wonderful food," said Keira, "And to answer your question, we are indeed on a pilgrimage of sorts."

Isamu took a seat at the end of the log as he stroked his long chin. "Then you must stay here the night and rest. We don't have much, but what we have, we share. Besides, it's not often we get visitors."

Nishi's eyes widened. It wasn't much, and if Aya hadn't been paying attention, she might have missed it.

Keira took a large bite out of her meat, oblivious to anything.

Aya turned to Isamu. "But your wife told us that you get refugees passing through here all the time."

Isamu coughed loudly as he struggled to clear his throat. He gazed at his wife, sweat pouring down his forehead.

"What my husband meant to say is that he's always out hunting. He's almost never here to meet the refugees who pass by."

"Yes," said Isamu. "That's it." He ate the rest of the meal without muttering a word. His wife did the same. This only served to heighten Aya's awkwardness.

"Can we play with the bear again, Mom?" asked Nari once they had finished their food.

"No. It's time to sleep."

"But, Mom, Loriko wants us to play with him, yes he does."

Nishi pointed toward the cabin. "To bed. Loriko will be here when you wake in the morning."

"Actually," said Aya. "I think we're going to keep on moving. We're in a hurry."

"Nonsense," said Keira. "We need to rest. What better place than with these fine folk?"

Nishi and Isamu both bobbed their heads. "Yes. That is for the best. It is almost night, and we have an extra room you may share."

Now it was Aya's turn to force a smile as the cool air messed with her hair. Even as she followed Keira and Loriko into the cabin, she couldn't shake her growing doubts about the family's hospitality.

"You're crazy," said Keira once Aya had revealed her suspicions. They were now in a room with two beds. Each girl took one of them while Loriko squeezed himself on the floor.

"Didn't you catch any of the signs?" said Aya, growing restless.

Keira threw herself on the bed. "There were no signs to catch."

"They had too much food for a simple family of four. Who else were they planning to feed?"

Keira narrowed her eyes. "Maybe they were really hungry."

"I think they may be working with your uncle. And I know they're hiding something. We should leave before we get a nasty surprise."

Keira blew out the candle atop the middle drawer. The room was immediately engulfed in darkness. "Try to get some sleep, will you?"

But Aya could not sleep. Even after Loriko's loud snores settled in, she remained awake. She strained her ears, waiting for the sound of imperial horses or soldiers, but nothing came. After hours of silence, she began to think that maybe she was going a bit mad. She allowed her eyes to close and her mind to wander. That's when she heard the soft whispers. They weren't too loud, but they were definitely there. She tiptoed toward the door and snuck out to the living room. Yuto and Nari lay sprawled on the floor, deep in sleep.

The morning sun blinded her as she opened the front door. How long was I awake for? Ignoring her tired body, she followed the hushed whispers to the back of the cabin. As she turned the corner she ran into a group of people who definitely were not soldiers.

They were about two dozen men, women, and children. They wore old, ragged clothing. All of their faces were full of grime, as if they had been underground for a long time.

"We've been discovered!" shrieked a stubby woman as her eyes settled on Aya.

Isamu ran in front of the people and held his hands out. "Get back, spy. We won't allow you to take these people."

Spy. "What are you talking about?"

"We know who you are," added Nishi. "You're working with that monster, Hotaru. Well we won't allow you to continue your oppression. Can't you see they just want to live their lives in peace?"

Aya shook her head, unable to take in the strange turn of events. "I'm no spy."

"Of course you are," said Nishi. "You're a Rohad. Do you think we don't know that the Rohads sided with Hotaru and helped murder Emperor Takumi?"

"That wasn't me," said Aya, growing restless. How many times was she going to be accused for something she didn't do?

"What is going on here?" Keira staggered behind Aya, rubbing her eyes. "I was trying to nap, but the ruckus you were all making made it impossible." Loriko followed behind her.

"Highness," cried the stubby woman. She ran to Keira and gave her a slight bow as she wiped away her tears. "You're alive. We thought you were dead."

The rest of the people flocked around Keira.

Nishi and Isamu stood frozen, their mouths wide open.

Keira stared at the crowd of people, her mouth gaping. "Are you all fleeing from my uncle?"

The people nodded.

"We had no idea you were the princess," said Nishi. "You see, we don't go to the city much. Had we known, we would have treated you with proper respect."

Keira held up her hand. "You welcomed me into your home and shared your food. And you're looking out for my people by hiding them from that tyrant. You have shown me enough respect to last a lifetime." She held both their hands. "Rest assured, once I reclaim my father's city, you will be properly rewarded."

The people cheered at the news, which brought a large grin to Keira's face. And even after they had said their goodbyes and continued on their trek, the grin remained.

"You were right," said Keira after a few minutes of walking. "They were evil masterminds plotting to turn us over to my uncle."

"Well, I was right about them hiding something," said Aya, though she couldn't shake the feeling of failure that loomed over her. In less than a day her instincts had failed her twice.

They moved for many hours in silence. The scenery remained the same, countless trees, leaves, and plants. Finally, when the sun was close to descending behind the green mountains, the bear stopped, his eyes darting about.

"I sense it too," said Aya, hoping she was just imagining the gaze she felt coming from the large bushel of leaves before them. Though she was certain she wasn't.

Seconds later, a four-legged silhouette emerged from the darkness in front of her. The shadow moved forward, revealing a yellow, reptilian-skinned jaguar. It opened its mouth. A set of hungry, razor-sharp fangs loomed closer.

Instantly the white bear stood on its two hind legs, covering Keira behind its shadow.

Aya gulped as she took out her batons. Loriko was still injured from the fall he'd sustained. He was in no shape to take on a jaguar.

"Move behind me," ordered Aya. "I can hold it back while…aaargh—" A sharp pain burst on her kneecap. She looked down just in time to see Keira hit her with a branch on her shin. Heart racing, Aya crumpled to the floor. "What are you doing!?"

"Let's go, Loriko," ordered Keira, stumbling as she took off in full retreat. "With the jaguar busy with the mercenary, we can escape."

The bear turned to her master, hesitant to leave.

"I said, let's go!"

This time the bear took off ahead of its master, leaving nothing in between the water wielder and the vicious feline.

Still on the ground, Aya took hold of her weapons, just as the jaguar pounced on her.

CHAPTER 19

The wind carried the smell of wet dirt as Falcon readied himself. He brought the sword over his head, sizing up the old man before him. He took off in a full sprint, lifting a wave of leaves behind him.

"Go, Falcon!" cheered Iris, who sat beside Faith under a prairie tree.

Falcon continued forward, his sword now a moment away from striking the chaos wielder.

"Wait," said Demetrius, holding his hand up.

Falcon's heart froze as he stopped the sword mere inches away from Demetrius. "Why didn't you dodge?"

"No need to, I knew you would stop." He held out his hands and rotated them in a circular motion. "I beg your pardon. But I have to stretch. You understand. The muscles of a poor old man are not as strong as they once were."

"Yes, of course," said Falcon. He waited as Demetrius stretched what seemed every part of his body. The fresh breeze coursed around Falcon as the minutes trickled by. Finally, after what seemed like hours, the chaos wielder stopped.

"Good. I believe I'm ready now."

Without saying a word, Falcon brought up his katana and rushed forward.

Demetrius' hand shot up again. "Wait!"

"What is it now?" said Falcon, stopping in mid-sprint.

"This sun is blinding me." He put up his hands to cover his eyes. "Perhaps we could switch spots."

Falcon moved to where Demetrius had been standing. He looked up at the sky, sighing as he noticed the sun was barely even visible from behind a large cloud.

Falcon rushed forward.

"Halt!"

Falcon took a frustrated breath. "What now?"

Demetrius reached into his ragged sandal and chuckled. "There is a little something bothering me." After seconds of searching he pulled out a small pebble and tossed it aside. "Funny how the smallest things can cause the greatest discomfort."

"Yes, yes. Let's go. I'm here to train."

Demetrius winced. "So quick to rush. Tell me. What do you know about control?"

"A lot," said Falcon. "Now let's go."

"It sure doesn't seem that way."

Falcon's ears grew warm. "I'll show you." Falcon swung his sword where the old man stood. The weapon cut only air.

"You're going to have to be faster than that if you want to show me what you learned."

"C'mon, Falcon." Iris hopped in place. "You can do it."

Falcon clenched his teeth. Chaos teleportation, of course. He moved for another attack. Again, his weapon whooshed through the air, hitting nothing.

"This is getting tiresome," said Demetrius. This time he stood at Falcon's right side. "Are you ever going to land a hit on my amazing face?"

The pit in Falcon's stomach intensified with heat. He felt his skin hardening. He was changing, changing into that monster from before.

Suddenly, Demetrius appeared directly in front of him. His skin was a dark brown. His regular eyes were gone, replaced instead with hollowed yellow pits. "Did you think you were the only one who could call on chaos form?"

Falcon staggered back. A pair of hands held him, bringing him back to reality. When he looked up, he noticed that the old man was back to his old self as well.

Faith stood behind Falcon, her hands surrounded by a white aura.

"You have a lot of anger, youngling." Demetrius took a seat beside Iris. "Much more than I've seen anyone have."

"I've been through a lot," said Falcon, letting Faith's holy energy flow through him.

Faith removed her hands. "We all have."

"Truer words have never been spoken," said Demetrius. "Every person goes through their own set of trials and tribulations. It's how we react to it that makes us who we are." The old man brought his hand to his chin. It remained there as he hummed to himself, lost in thought. "The truth is that you have too much energy. The more chaos you have, the angrier you're prone to get."

Falcon thought back to the words of the Ghost Knight. "I was once told to use the people I care for as a shield to suppress my anger."

"That is a good beginning, but you need more. You must find a way to control it. It is something I cannot teach you."

Falcon's spirits dwindled into nothingness. How was he supposed to defeat Shal-Volcseck and find his lost brother if he couldn't even control himself?

"But I know someone who can. To combat such ferocity, viciousness, and rage, you need equal levels of love, harmony, and serenity." The chaos wielder turned to Faith. "What you need is a holy wielder."

~~~

"Maybe it's my fault," said Faith after Falcon failed to create yet another holy shield. Iris and Father Lucien sat far away under a tree, busily eating bread and apples out of a basket. Shal-Demetrius stood, watching over them. "I've never trained anyone before. I don't even know if I'm doing it right."

"You're doing just fine," said Demetrius. He took a step toward them. "Continue trying, I'm sure you'll get it."

Falcon repeated the same set of movements he'd been doing for the past two weeks. His eyes closed. He brought his hands slowly up, as if in prayer.

Nothing.

Besides the frustration at his inability to control holy, he felt empty.

"I can't do it on my own," he whined. "When I feel Faith's touch I can sense the holy energy flowing inside of me, but on my own I simply can't."

"What can I do, Demetrius?" Faith asked. She seemed as lost as Falcon.

"Well, I'm not sure what you can do. But I'm going to go eat some of those salamis your friends over there are eating. I haven't had any in forever."

Falcon staggered. "Is this a joke to you? I can't kill Volcseck if I don't become stronger."

"And it's possible holy wielding is not even the answer," added Faith.

Demetrius stopped and turned toward Falcon. His face grew stern. "I used to be much like you, youngling. Always rushing into battle, never thinking things through. That is, until I met her."

"Her?" whispered Faith.

"Yes. She was a holy wielder. Her name was Lunet." Demetrius paused for a second. "And she was my wife."

"You knew a holy wielder?" asked Faith, her voice filled with shock. "That's amazing. I knew there had been other ones. I just never heard of any."

The old man grimaced as he took Faith's hand. "She was a beauty. Not until I met you have I known someone who had so much compassion in their heart. 'Love can conquer all,' she would always say."

Faith's expression softened.

"She made a better man out of me," continued Demetrius. "I'm sure you can do the same for this rascal."

Faith's eyes brightened up. "That's it."

Demetrius unexpectedly turned and took off in a mad sprint toward Father Lucien and Iris, yelling and waving at them to save some food for him.

~~~

Faith smiled inwardly, feeling sure of what she had to do.

"That was strange," said Falcon. "One minute he's sad, the other he's going nuts over sausage."

Faith took in the smell of the salted meat. She moved in front of Falcon and stared into his eyes.

"What is it?" said Falcon.

Faith thought back to the years she had passed alone in the woods, repeatedly practicing the same routines until they were ingrained in her mind. "I wasted a lot of time when I was trying to develop my holy wielding."

217

"That's understandable. It's not like you ever had a master to teach you."

"It was not until I thought back to the people in the village and my love for them that I finally developed the holy shield."

Falcon grimaced.

"So far you've used the people you care about as a barrier to somewhat control your emotions, but you're going to have to take it farther than that." Faith grinned. "You're going to have to find something that you love."

CHAPTER 20

As he entered the woodsy area, Falcon felt eyes watching him. He searched the trees, attempting to lock down the energy readings. He sensed the power all around him. In the trees, the grass beneath his feet, even in the small insects that scurried over a dead log at his side.

"I can't do it!" he said, throwing his hands up in frustration. "Every time I try I sense the energy all over the place. I can't lock it down."

Suddenly, Shal-Demetrius and Faith appeared before him in a puff of smoke.

"It's okay," said Faith sweetly. "I'm sure you'll get it soon enough."

"Um hum." Demetrius cleared his throat. For a moment, he glared at Faith, as if expecting her to say something else.

"Yes, sir?" asked Faith, her voice low.

"What is it that we spoke about, young holy wielder?" asked Demetrius "You must be more assertive. Don't baby him. He will never learn that way."

Faith nodded shyly. "Um...yes. More assertive." She looked directly at Falcon's eyes. For a moment, she looked lost, as if unsure of what to do. "Falcon. Um...you must try really, really hard."

The forest grew quiet. Falcon smirked. She was trying very hard, but being bossy was obviously not her forte.

"That's it?" asked Demetrius, taken aback.

"And do it quickly," Faith whimpered.

Demetrius brought his hand to his forehead and sighed. "Well. Maybe ordering people around is not for you. Nonetheless, your idea about love is not to be ignored. There is promise there."

"I don't know," Falcon said tentatively. He wasn't fond of sharing his emotions with anyone. Better to keep them locked inside where they belonged. "Maybe we should find another way."

Demetrius nodded. "Like what? Should you just always wait for the power to simply somehow conveniently come to you in times of need?" Sarcasm dripped from his voice.

"It worked before." Falcon recalled a few of those times. "When I battled Lao, I managed to keep control of all the basic elements. Then there was this—"

"Stop right there," said Demetrius. "I'm not interested in occasions where you magically got control of your power." The chaos wielder waved his hands around mockingly. "That's called dumb luck and adrenaline. What you need is to grasp control of it so that you manage it at will. So time to speak up. What are the strongest emotions of love you have?"

Falcon gulped loudly as he pulled as his collar. "There must be another way."

"Falcon. Just go with the procedure." Faith stared at him, fire in her eyes.

"Well, well." Demetrius nodded. "What do we have here? Finally some spunk from the holy wielder."

A pained look came over Faith, as if she regretted her words. "I'm sorry, Falcon. I didn't mean to talk to you that way. I'm just trying to help."

"Don't apologize!" cried Demetrius.

"It was you and Aya," admitted Falcon, his stomach lurching. His friend was obviously trying hard, giving it her all for his training. He, at least, owed her an equal effort as well.

"Aya and me what?" asked Faith, obviously still confused.

His voice grew shakier. "I was er…thinking of you and Aya when I took control of all the elements. I…I didn't want to lose you both."

Faith's face turned a deep red. "Oh. Sorry. I didn't mean to—"

The only one who seemed to be having the time of his life was Demetrius. He clapped his hands loudly and grinned. "Now we're getting somewhere. See? Was that so hard?"

Yes, thought Falcon, still embarrassed.

"Now," continued Demetrius, "I'm going to take Faith's hand once again. As soon as I do, I will chaos teleport her somewhere in the vicinity. It is your job to pinpoint our energy and teleport to us. Got it?"

"Yes." Falcon nodded, glad he didn't have to face Faith a second longer.

The chaos wielder took the hand of the holy wielder. In a puff of smoke, they were gone.

Falcon closed his eyes, focused on Faith and Aya, and returned to his search.

CHAPTER 21

Aya stumbled back, her eyes scanning the reptilian-skinned jaguar. She noticed the yellow, glossy skin and the black spots dotted throughout its body. Judging from the two long fangs at each side of its mouth, and its long, muscular body, she was certain she was dealing with a female chilera. She'd read about them many times in her study books. She had just never thought she would come face to face with one.

The chilera gritted her teeth, exposing an even set of sharp fangs. She brought her upper body down, and pounced.

Aya clicked the stick hanging by her waist. Instantly it extended to become her blue baton. As the chilera neared her, she moved back and brought it down. The baton slammed on the animal's skull.

The beast craned her neck and took a bite. Aya took another step back, and it only tasted air.

Aya steadied her breath as the chilera moved around her. She knew any mistake could mean her life. With a high-pitched growl, it zigzagged as it dashed toward her.

Aya darted her eyes, ready for any time it might pounce, but instead it staggered back, growling under its breath.

Aya recognized what the chilera was doing. The books back at Rohad mentioned their tendency to circle their victims, feigning attacks for hours until their prey tired. Then, and only then, would they attack.

We'll see about that. Aya unclicked her second baton. She huffed as she released the first baton with all her force. As the chilera moved back to avoid the attack, Aya dashed forward. She came in front of the animal and brought down her remaining weapon. As it moved in for a desperate bite, Aya flipped the baton around and rammed the end into the animal's expecting mouth. As it staggered back, Aya brought her knuckles directly on the chilera's neck. The animal crashed to the dirt with a loud yelp.

"See?" said Aya, leaning down and running her hand over the chilera's smooth skin. "You should stick to eating birds and squirrels. Attacking humans is liable to get you killed."

The beast moved her fearful eyes toward Aya as it lay uselessly on the ground.

Aya clicked her batons back into place. "Don't worry, I'm not going to kill you. And I'll take off the paralysis in a minute." She patted the chilera's belly. The roundness of it confirmed her suspicion. "So you're pregnant. I knew you wouldn't attack if you weren't desperate." She took out a large chunk of dry meat she had hoped to eat later on her travels and set it in front of the animal.

Aya met the chilera's eyes. "Now listen. No more attacking, got it?" The chilera whimpered. Trusting her instincts, Aya knuckled her fist and pressed on the nerve again.

The beast stood and picked up the chunk of meat. With the slab still in its mouth, it looked one last time at Aya. It lowered its gaze and took off into the forest.

Aya didn't know if she was crazy or if talking to Faith had gotten to her, but she could have sworn she saw gratitude in the animal's eyes.

~~~

A wave of heat washed over Aya as she moved about the forest. Light trickled though the thick branches above. She'd been walking for over two weeks now, following the tracks Keira and Loriko had left behind.

She was growing frustrated and worried. Over the past few hours the tracks had grown erratic. They weren't headed toward the meeting grounds, but away from them. Not only that, but the paw prints had been replaced with long stretches of smoothed ground, as if someone had been dragged.

She followed the zigzagging tracks a few more hours, wondering how a forest that was covered with so much shade could possibly be this hot and humid.

"Rrrrrrrrr!"

Aya froze in her tracks, certain that that had been an animal roar. Could it be another chilera?

"Rrrrrrrrr!"

No. The jaguar's roar had a much lower tone. This growl was much more savage. Her hopes spiked.

She waited patiently for it to come again.

"Rrrrrrrrr!"

To the right.

She moved with renewed vigor. Every branch, leaf, and plant that got in her way was quickly tossed aside in her haste.

"Rrrrrrrrr!"

"Kahito Lemuel. Yuri. Kahito!"

Aya tried to make sense of the words being spoken.

"Kahito. Lemruata."

She grimaced. The language was alien and strange to her. A few steps later she found that that wasn't the only strange thing.

From her hiding spot behind a bush, Aya noticed a series of palm-leaved huts lined up in a straight line. There were a number of large pots boiling over small flames. Dozens of tan-skinned men, wearing only loincloths, moved about. Most of them had paintings on their faces, chest, and backs. Some had bones pierced through their noses and lips. But what caught Aya's attention wasn't the wild-looking men, or the fact that dozens of human bones lay scattered about.

Her eyes instead focused on the two nets hanging at the middle of the camp. Loriko hung in the large net, snarling at the men with wooden spears circling him. Keira hung in the

226

other net. Even from afar, Aya noticed the slight tremble in her lips.

"Lorues Kohitu," said a man who sat on a chair at the end of the camp. He held a human skull on his hands, which he used to take sips out of. The purple liquid that didn't make it inside his mouth ran down his jaw and neck. "Lorues Kohito!"

At this last command the men with the spears backed off, leaving Loriko alone.

Aya didn't understand the words they spoke, but there were two things that she had already surmised. First, the man using the skull as his own personal tumbler was the leader. Second, judging from all the bones and the man's cup, these people were cannibals. Which meant the next thing on the menu was Keira.

Doesn't matter. They won't get to her as long as I'm patient. She settled down and looked on for what seemed an eternity.

Finally, when the bloodred moon had been out for hours, the chief stood from the chair he'd been sitting in all day. He belched loudly as he tossed a human arm he had been taking bites out of to the side. He moved over to Keira, who still had a slight tremble.

"Totuy. Totuy," said the man, pointing at his blind prisoner and licking his dark lips.

Aya readied herself as the anxiety in her insides grew. Is he going to kill her now?

But seconds later the chief laughed and trudged over to the largest hut at the end of the camp. Taking a cue from their leader, the other savages went into huts of their own. Only two men remained sitting on a log, keeping watch on their future meal.

Aya's anxiety subsided a bit. It appeared that Keira was still not on the menu.

Aya waited a few more hours. She had to make sure that the camp was asleep before she made her move. When the moon reached the center of the sky, she decided that it was time.

Crouching, she stepped out of the bushes. Her hunting instincts kicked in as she gingerly moved toward the captives.

One of the guards lay on the ground, snoring loudly. The other sat on the log, his body wobbling as he struggled to keep his eyes open.

Aya came behind him and brought her hands around his neck. She pressed down hard. The Nakatomi lock was near impossible to escape; her perfect form made sure of that.

Seconds later, she set the unconscious man quietly on the ground.

The second man's eyes snapped open. A quick open-fisted hit to his cranium put him back to sleep.

"What are you doing here?" whispered Keira, seemingly barely noticing Aya.

"Saving you. What else does it look like?"

"B...but how did you escape the jaguar? You couldn't even wield."

"With difficulty," said Aya, pulling out a small dagger. "Though I don't think this is the time to be discussing that."

The blind girl remained quiet as Aya worked the rope. A minute later she crashed to the ground.

Aya held her breath, waiting for any sign from inside the huts signifying that they'd been heard. After a minute of silence, Aya moved to the larger net.

She suppressed a sigh of worry as she noticed the deep, bloody cuts on Loriko's leg and paw.

"It's fine," said Keira, noticing Aya's concern. "Those savages hurt us when they captured us, but my bears are tough. They can run even with injuries like those."

Aya nodded and went to work on Loriko's net. Moments later, the rope ripped, sending the heavy animal crashing to the ground. It landed on its injured hind leg.

"Grrrrrrrr!"

"Oh, no," cried Aya. "We have to get a move on. There is no way they did not hear that."

The bear struggled to its feet.

Aya took Keira's hand and helped her up. "Move. Now!"

"There's a way out this way," said Keira. She pointed to a barely visible dirt path behind the last hut.

Keira took point. Aya followed behind. Loriko brought up the rear.

The cries of angry men filled the night air as they moved out of the collection of huts.

"They're coming after us!" said Keira, huffing loudly. "Bridge up ahead. Almost there."

Aya looked past Keira and to the bear. With every step he took, blood spilled to the dirt below. She could only imagine the pain it was causing to put weight on his injured legs, but despite the gruesome injury, his pace remained constant.

"Keaul. Luterid. Luta!"

Aya turned and her mouth dried. Closing behind her were countless spear-wielding men. They were still a distance away, but at their pace, she was sure they would be on top of them in no time.

"There's the bridge!" Keira cried.

"Kuaul. Kuaul!" The screams got louder by the second.

Aya and Keira stepped into the wooden bridge. It rocked dangerously as the girls dashed across it.

Aya gulped as she noticed the sheer fall that awaited her if she took a wrong step. Her jaw did not unclench until they had set foot on the other side of the bridge.

"C'mon, Loriko!" cried Keira at the bear who still stood at the other side of the bridge. "We're across, so you don't have to worry about putting too much weight on the—"

Loriko turned to them. He held his clawed hand up in the air, swinging it forward and ripping the rope that held the bridge.

"Ahhh…Loriko?" Keira stood motionless, as her voice became a squeak. "What are you doing?"

Loriko stood on his hand legs and roared.

"He's saving us," said Aya.

Keira remained in place. "No. I will not leave her to die."

Now it was Aya who stood in shock. Loriko is a girl?

The next few events transpired in seconds.

Loriko rushed the dozen weapon-holding silhouettes. From afar, Aya said a silent prayer as the large shadow engulfed half a dozen men. Maybe there was hope for her after all.

A second later Aya's hope shattered as a silhouette snuck behind Loriko and dug its spear in her back.

"Gota. Gota!"

Aya recognized the voice as that of the chief's.

Loriko turned and delivered a vicious swing of her paw, sending the chief to the floor. His head landed a foot away from his body.

The savages dug their spears into Loriko, each attack sending a roar of pain through the air.

"My friend!" cried Keira between sobs. She rushed toward the cliff. "Lori!"

Aya jumped and held her back.

Keira struggled to break free. "Let me go. S…she needs me!"

Aya fell to the ground with Keira, refusing to release her. She sadly gazed at Lori, wishing she could help.

Lori beat down the last of her attackers. Then her silhouette stumbled to the ground, releasing a mushroom of dust around her. Half a dozen spears penetrated her back. Lori lifted her head. Her last tired, low whimper moved through the air.

A second later her head crashed, and her movement ceased.

CHAPTER 22

"Like this?" asked Falcon as he dug his feet into the sand.

Demetrius cast another line into the crystal-clear lake. He swung his wobbly fishing rod around, as if that would change his luck.

Falcon sighed in frustration. "Demetrius? Am I doing the technique right or not? I'm never going to learn how to teleport if you never teach me."

"I am teaching you, youngling," said Demetrius, not bothering to turn toward the young wielder. He reached into his bucket and pulled out another worm. Ever so carefully he set the worm in the hook and threw it into the lake again. "With this bait, I'm sure I'll catch a delicious meal for us."

"I don't care about meals. I need to know how to teleport if I'm going to bring in Lakirk for questioning. I'm sure he has been aided by Volcseck, and I'm going to capture him and make him reveal his whereabouts."

"Then you should stop talking and concentrate on the task at hand."

"Yes, but I need more to go on than 'close your eyes and think'."

Demetrius walked to the basket he'd set up by the water and took out a large pichion egg. He tossed it at his pupil.

Falcon caught the egg and shrugged. "What am I supposed to do with this?"

After a minute of Demetrius holding his finger to his chin, he held his head up. "Aha. I got it. I want you to bring one leg up, so that you're only standing on one leg."

"Like this?" asked Falcon, lifting his right leg.

"Yes, that's good. Now set the egg down on your knee and hold that pose as long as you can."

"Er...okay." Falcon carefully put the egg on his lifted knee. He took a deep breath as he remained ramrod straight. He didn't see the purpose of the exercise, but Demetrius was a master. He was certain he had a reason.

Demetrius looked on with admiration. "Not bad." He poked Falcon's stomach a few times, causing him to wobble slightly. "You have strong legs. But chaos requires more than physical power. I want you to close your eyes and concentrate on your family."

"I don't have any fami—"

"Shhh.... Don't speak, simply concentrate."

Falcon closed his eyes. He vaguely made out the sound of Demetrius casting his fishing rod into the water again. But in moments, every outside noise was drowned out by the sound of water splashing. He looked on as his mother stumbled toward him.

"Mother!" cried Falcon inside his head. He reached for her, but as he did, a bloodied sword appeared through her stomach.

"Why didn't you save me?" she asked. "You hid behind a bush as I died. How could you be so cowardly?"

A lump formed in his throat as he tried to say the right words, but nothing came.

"Weak coward, weak coward, weak coward."

His mother disappeared, replaced by the sight of his father, Anson. He looked down on him with fierce eyes. "You could have saved her, but you didn't. I'm ashamed to call you my son, you spineless worm."

A spear appeared out of seemingly nowhere and pierced his father's head. As the spear dug into the skull, the image of Anson dissolved into a black mist.

"Hello, brother," said Albert.

Falcon staggered back. "A...a-albert?" He had on the same brown tunic he'd worn the last time Falcon had seen him.

"You don't want to believe that I murdered the council. But the truth is that I did. I craved power. I wanted it so bad I could taste it. Unlimited power. There is nothing better."

"No. This is not real."

"I'm as real as you. And like you, I'm a monster too. No, what am I saying? You're the real monster here. You are the chaos wielder, after all."

"Shut up! Just shut—" Falcon closed his mouth as he took a step back. No. I need to take control. I must not give in.

"Don't shove me away," said Albert. "I'm your brother, your own flesh and blood. Don't you want to be like me?"

"You're no brother of mine. You're the chaos inside of me." He envisioned a barrier in his mind. With great effort he brought his trembling hands together as a golden ring encircled his brother. The ring shrank in size, squeezing the life out of Albert.

His brother held out his hand. "You can't do this to me. You can't do this."

Falcon's eyes snapped open. He wiped his sweaty hands on his shirt. His leg was still up, and the egg safely rested on his knee. "I did it!"

"Did what?" asked Demetrius, pulling his string of bait through the lake.

"I controlled the chaos. I thought you were crazy with your methods, but it actually worked." In his excitement he forgot to set his foot down.

"No!" cried Demetrius as the egg rolled down Falcon's leg and to the ground. It shattered loudly atop a rock. "I was going to eat that with my fish."

Falcon scratched his chin. "Sorry."

236

~~~

"Thank you," said Faith as the lady handed her a loaf of bread. She took a whiff of the blueberry wheat and set it in her basket.

"I got the potato." Iris held the vegetable over her head. "The man gave me a discount because he knows I'm with you."

"That was nice of him. Did you say thank you?"

"Of course, Faith. I haven't forgotten what you taught me."

Faith took the girl's hand and led her down the path into the forest. "That's good."

Iris smiled. "Do you think Falcon and the old geezer have made any progress in the training?"

"Iris!"

"Oh. Sorry. I meant to say Mr. Demetrius, not old geezer."

"That's better." Faith took in the fresh breeze that coursed through the air. It reminded her of her home, Asturia. "And as for Falcon, I'm sure he's doing fine. He's very good."

"But he gets angry quickly, doesn't he?"

Faith glanced at Iris, admiring her awareness. "Yes, he has a hard time staying in control sometimes. But he does a good job at it, despite what he thinks. He…" She took a deep breath. "He doesn't hate me after what I did to him."

Iris's eyes narrowed and her steps slowed. "What did you do?"

Faith felt an ache in her chest as she forced the words out of her mouth. "Falcon's parents died because of me."

"Really?"

"Shal-Volcseck attacked my village because he was looking for me. It was during this attack that both his parents were killed." Faith took another breath, attempting to keep steady. "It's all my fault; and yet, he's never been unkind to me. On the contrary, he's been the total opposite of that. So you see? He is kind despite the chaos inside of him. He just has a hard time seeing it sometimes, that's all."

"Yes. I'm sure you're right."

"How about you, Iris? I told you a little about me, but I still don't know much about you."

Iris dragged her feet as a slight frown formed on her lips. "Not much to say. I was found as a baby at the doorsteps of the infirmary. The nurses looked after me until I was three. Then all of them left to the capital cities. Since then, I have been on my own."

Faith felt a knot form in her stomach. "How did you survive?"

"People always throw away scraps of food, especially during the holidays. I also started offering my services as a guide to K'vitch. That got me a few coins to keep me fed once in a while. That is how I found you."

"And I'm so glad you did," said Faith. "I promise you that you're never going to have to eat out of trashcans again. I'll see to that."

Iris squeezed Faith's hand tighter. "Thank you. That means so much to me."

"No!" A cry echoed in the air.

Iris's head darted about. "What was that?"

"It sounded like it came from the lake," said Faith. "C'mon, let's go see if everything is fine."

The girls hurried down the path. It led them around a large rock, beneath a wooden bridge, and out into the yellow sand.

Demetrius was on his knees. "No, my egg!"

"Don't worry," said Faith. She lifted the basket of eggs. "I got plenty here."

Demetrius smiled. "Great job, youngling." He stood and returned to his fishing rod. "All I need now is to catch a fish and I can have my sandwich."

Falcon shrugged as he stared at Faith. "I actually managed to control some of the chaos, but he's more excited about eggs."

"That's great, Falcon!" shrieked Faith. "That's such a good step for you. I knew having someone who knows your element would help."

"How did you do it?" asked Iris excitedly.

Falcon took an egg from the basket and raised his knee. Taking great care, he set the egg on his knee.

Faith wore a face of confusion. "Is that really necessary?"

"Yes, according to Demetrius. It's a way to keep me focused physically and mentally."

Demetrius snickered loudly to himself. "I'm afraid you're overthinking things a bit, youngling."

Falcon handed the egg back to Faith. "What do you mean?"

"The only reason I had you hold the egg like that was because I thought it would be funny to see you struggling to keep your balance. I was getting bored and I needed some form of entertainment."

Falcon's jaw dropped. "So that was for nothing?"

"No, not for nothing. Weren't you listening? It was to give me a good laugh."

"Do it again, Falcon," said Iris between giggles. "Do it again. I want to see you fall and break an egg."

Falcon licked his teeth, unable to believe he'd fallen for the old man's trick. "You know, you're not at all what I expected."

"And what did you expect, youngling? You thought that because I was a chaos wielder I was going to be silent, brooding, and humorless?"

"Well, yes, actually."

Demetrius grinned, exposing crooked dark teeth. "You would do well to not pass judgment on people simply by the title they carry."

Falcon's thoughts drifted back to Aya and the day he'd met her. "A friend told me that once too."

"I got one!" cried Demetrius as he pulled the rod back. A squirming gray fish landed on the sand. The old man rubbed his stomach. "Sandwich time!"

Falcon grinned. Yes, indeed, this man was not what he had expected. But that didn't necessarily seem like a bad thing anymore.

CHAPTER 23

Falcon took in the aroma of the sweet bread as he stuffed it in his mouth. The egg inside it melted on his tongue, causing him to sigh with satisfaction. At first he had thought this night picnic to be a bad idea, but now he wasn't too sure.

"Falcon!" said Faith, looking absolutely aghast. "I had no idea you could eat like that."

Iris too stood with mouth wide open. "I suppose he was very hungry."

"A man with no patience with food is also a man with no food," said Father Lucien. "And a man with no food can never watch the birds fly."

"That's very true," said Shal-Demetrius. He leaned on the thick branch of the tree.

Falcon felt his cheeks redden as he forced the food down his throat. "I'm sorry, Faith."

"Sorry?" asked Faith. "Don't be. It's fine. I was just a bit shocked to see you eat with such ferocity. That's all." She returned to braiding Iris's long hair. "It's actually kind of funny. I never have seen you act that way."

Iris, who sat cross-legged in front of a kneeling Faith, caressed the ponytail that had been finished. "Wow. It's so shiny."

Faith ran more water through the girl's hair. "It's amazing what a little wash can do."

Falcon nodded. He had to agree. Iris did look much better now that Faith had washed her in the lake.

All of a sudden, Iris clasped Faith's hand. A silent tear dripped out from her eye as her gaze remained locked on Falcon's. "You two have been so kind to me. No one has ever treated me this way. No one." The girl's voice was full of sadness and gratitude. "Th...thanks so much for saving me, for everything. I don't deserve—"

Faith held the girl in her arms. "Don't you say that. Of course you deserve it. You're an amazing person." She looked up at Falcon, her eyes demanding that he say something.

Falcon, not sure what to say, cleared his throat. "Um...that's right. You deserve the best."

The little girl remained sobbing quietly while Faith held her tight.

"Not that great with words, huh?" said Father Lucien. "Have you figured out my little riddle from back on our wagon ride?"

Falcon sighed, not sure why Faith had insisted on bringing the father along. "No, I can't say that I have."

"Perhaps if you spent less time thinking about your sword and wielding and more about words and their meaning, you would make some progress."

"Can we get back to training?" asked Falcon.

243

"In your case this is training," Demetrius said. "Learning to relax is a virtue you would do well to remember. Besides, the moon has just passed the middle of the sky. We should have gone to sleep hours ago."

"I'm not sleepy."

"Then meditate."

"Meditation never helped me get any answers before. I doubt it will now."

"Is that so?" asked the chaos wielder. He took a seat in front of Falcon.

"What are you doing?" asked Falcon as Demetrius took his hand.

"Shush and close your eyes."

"But—"

"Do it!" Demetrius turned to Faith. "Could you join us as well?"

Faith appeared as confused as Falcon, but she remained silent as she put her hands over Falcon's.

Falcon closed his eyes. At first he saw nothing. Felt nothing. But after a few seconds, the wrinkled hands of Demetrius grew warm. Then he saw it.

He now stood in front of a small cottage. The fields around it as well as the pine trees were covered in snow. A tall man with sharp features stood at the door, apparently unaware that Falcon was watching him.

"Be gone, boy," ordered the man to a kid who couldn't be more than eight years of age. "The winters in these mountains are harsh. My wife and I barely have enough for ourselves. We can't share our morsels with any stray who comes calling."

"Demetrius!" A beautiful, red-haired woman called as he came out from inside the hut.

So the man is Demetrius. But why is he showing me something that happened so long ago?

"Yes, Lunet?"

The woman put her hand over a bloodied gash the boy had on his neck. The holy pearl on her hand brightened as the cut closed, leaving no sign of an injury. She took hold of the malnourished boy and led him into the cabin. "We always have room for those in need."

Demetrius took in a deep breath and held it. "Of course, dear."

"What is your name?" asked Lunet.

The boy looked up at the woman. He rubbed his bony cheeks. "Volcseck. My name is Volcseck."

A tornado slammed into the scene, carrying the images away. A moment later Falcon stood by a lake. Before him, Demetrius towered over a young man who couldn't be a day past twenty seasons old.

"Come at me, Volcseck."

Volcseck grinned as he unsheathed his sword. His cheeks looked much fuller now, and the dark bags under his eyes were nonexistent. He rushed forward with a flurry of sword strikes.

Falcon nodded with admiration. Both warriors moved with precision. Every attack, every feint, every parry was perfect, with no visible openings.

"Good. Good," said Demetrius, putting his sword away. Volcseck did the same. "You've done well these past few years. I believe you're ready."

"Yes!" cried Volcseck. He ran to Lunet and picked her up by her waist. "Did you hear that, Mother? I'm finally going to learn the secrets of chaos."

"Not exactly," interrupted Demetrius. "I want you to go train with the monks of the mountain pass. There you will remain for five years, away from the worldly temptations. When you get back, then we'll discuss your chaos training."

Volcseck set Lunet down. "What?"

"You heard me."

"Five years." Volcseck's voice remained monotone, with no hint of emotion despite his obvious disappointment. "That is a complete waste of time. You said I have the gift of chaos, like you."

Demetrius frowned as he stared at his emblem. "Curse is more like it. This power is not to be taken lightly. It can consume you if left unchecked."

"But you turned out fine."

Demetrius took hold of Lunet's hand. "That is only because I had my soul mate to guide me."

"I can control it," said Volcseck through clenched teeth.

"I've raised you as my son!" declared Demetrius, his voice rising. "You will obey my command."

"This is complete rustada," hissed Volcseck.

"Mind your mouth!" thundered Demetrius.

"I apologize for my foul language, Mother." He turned and headed into the forest, mumbling under his breath. "If you won't teach me, then I'll discover the power of chaos myself."

"Get back here," ordered Demetrius as he headed after his pupil.

Lunet took hold of her husband's hand. "Give him some time to think."

"No. If he doesn't listen, I will—"

"Get in another shouting duel? That's not what he needs now. Let him mull things over. He'll come around."

The scene dissolved. Seemingly from nowhere, stone pyramids emerged. Countless bald-headed, robe-wearing monks lay on the cold stone. Their eyes remained open, though the life inside them had been extinguished.

"What have you done?" Demetrius demanded. He now had a peppered mustache and beard decorating his face.

"Took matters into my own hands," answered Volcseck. He wore a black cloak, obscuring his facial features.

"S…son," stuttered Lunet. She gasped as she took in the sight before her. "When the monk's scroll expressed concern over your actions, we thought they were exaggerating. Why did you do this?"

Volcseck laughed, a cruel cackle that echoed through the rainy night. "For the past five years I've been training. Honing my chaos. It speaks to me. Tells me what to do."

"Fool!" Demetrius said. "You let the chaos consume you."

"No. I became part of it. With this new power I will finally bring a new era unto this wicked world."

"Son," pleaded Lunet, clearly on the brink of tears. She reached for Volcseck's hand.

"No more son. The chaos demands the holy emblem. So I will take it now."

"Don't you dare." Demetrius stepped in front of Lunet.

"Oh, Master." The young wielder took a step forward. "You don't even have your weapon."

Demetrius' head trembled with fury. "I don't need steel to teach you the difference between a master and a pup."

Thunder clashed as both chaos wielders moved against each other.

Demetrius dodged the first blade attack. The second attack found only air as the master teleported behind his pupil. He grabbed him in a chokehold.

A teleport later and Volcseck stood safely away from Demetrius' hold.

Under Volcseck's hood, Falcon noticed a large-toothed grin as the bodies of the dead monks stood. Their lifeless heads hung down.

"You mastered that attack," said Demetrius, shock in his voice. "Now I know that you truly are lost."

Out of nowhere, a rainbow-colored shield encircled both chaos wielders.

"Both of you, stop this," Lunet demanded. She moved toward the young man. "Son, why didn't you come to me if you needed help?"

"Get back!" yelled Demetrius, breaking out of his shield and rushing toward his wife.

Volcseck broke free from his shield as well and drove his sword forward.

There was a spurt of blood as the long sword entered Lunet's chest.

A second later Demetrius' fist delivered a crushing blow to his pupil's jaw, sending him flying uselessly through the air.

"Stop," said Lunet, blood dripping from her mouth. Her emblem glowed brightly as she struggled to where her son lay.

"Yes, you still have enough energy to heal your injury," said a hopeful Demetrius.

Falcon watched in shock as the redhaired holy wielder set her hand on Volcseck's broken jaw, healing his wound.

"I forgive you, son." With those last words her lifeless body crumpled into her husband's arms.

"The holy emblem, I need it," said Volcseck. The bravado and confidence was now gone, replaced by a slight tremble in his voice.

Could it be that he cared for her?

Demetrius caressed his dead wife's short hair. "Why, my love? Why?"

"The emblem," repeated Volcseck.

Demetrius looked up with heated rage in his eyes. "It will never be yours. Never, you hear? I'll make sure of that." The red cracks in the master's emblem intensified as a shield surrounded him. At the same time his wife's body, as well as her emblem, dissolved into nothingness. Seconds later the chaos wielder had been fully engulfed in a clear shield.

Falcon's eyes snapped open. He was back at the picnic field.

Demetrius winked at him. "You see? Meditating can be the answer to many questions. If you give it a chance."

"I see," said Falcon, mouth wide open. Perhaps he was wrong about meditation after all.

"I felt a connection with her," mumbled Faith. "Thank you for that. It was an honor to get to know a little about my holy sister."

"She would have been glad to have you consider her a sister."

"I don't get it," Iris suddenly burst out. "I see how you got in the shield and all, but how'd you get so old in there?"

"Iris!" said Faith.

Iris looked down. "I'm sorry. I kind of touched your hand while you were in that trance and saw what you saw."

"It's fine," said Demetrius. "As for the answer to your question: Time crawls forward inside the shield. My plan was to encase my wife along with her shield. I did not anticipate that the shield energy would dissolve the emblem the way it did."

Iris put a stern face. "You used to be so serious."

"That I was, youngling. But being trapped all that time gave me a lot of time to think." The old man hopped to his feet. "And now I think it's time we go to sleep. Here I come, cold hard cave." He took off in a full sprint toward the cave at the top of the hill.

"There is a warm bed for you at the infirmary," Father Lucien called out.

"No need," yelled Demetrius, still running.

"I think he prefers the cold," said Faith.

Father Lucien nodded. "Well, not me." He took hold of Iris's hand. "Let's go. You played the day away, and it's hours past bedtime."

The father and the girl said their goodbyes and headed back to the town on the brick-paved path that led to the infirmary.

Falcon and Faith took the dirt path back to town. They would have to go through the woods, but the path would lead them directly to the inn.

"So did you ever figure out that riddle?" said Faith.

"No, but I don't think it matters much."

"I would disagree. I think figuring it out would be a good step toward your training."

Falcon nodded. "Then I'll try my best to figure it out, for you." He grinned. "You are my master, after all."

"Thanks." They remained quiet as they continued walking over the moon-drenched path. "So how about that other thing we spoke about?"

"Er...you mean that love thing?" Falcon stared into Faith's emerald eyes and gulped. "I...I'm not sure what I should think about that. I love a lot of things. My mom, Albert, Master K'ran, and—"

"Where is it?" came a strange voice. They both turned toward the voice. In front of them stood a skinny young man. He moved around a bush of flowers, poking his head between the leaves. "How am I supposed to ask her now?"

"Is everything fine?" asked Falcon, glad that he didn't have to continue with the conversation.

The man stared at them. "No. Nothing is fine. Tonight, on our anniversary, I was to ask my love to marry me." He waved at a girl who sat on a blanket atop a hill. The distance made her features barely visible.

"Are you well, my honey-dipped dumpling?" said the girl between giggles. "Come and share some of this strawberry wine with me."

The thin-mustached man cleared his throat. "Yes, my love. As soon as I find the perfect flower."

"Honey-dipped dumpling?" asked Falcon, trying his best to stifle his urge to laugh.

"Yes. What's wrong with that?"

"Nothing," interrupted Faith. "Now, what ails you, sir? Perhaps we can help."

"The ring," he whispered. "I had the perfect ring to ask her to spend her life with me. And I dropped it while I searched for a flower. Now I can't find it anywhere. It wasn't much, but it was all I could afford."

Faith took a red rose in her hand. The white emblem glowed as the stem shifted into a pristine gold ring. Small golden-colored leaves decorated the body of it. The red rose turned into a gleaming ruby gem. "Take it."

Falcon stood dumbfounded. He'd assumed holy wielding was only for healing and defensive spells. He never imagined it was capable of such things.

"Goodness sake," said the man. "I can't take this."

"Please. It would be my honor."

The man took the shimmering jewel in his hand. "My gratitude to you. I hope the love between you two is blessed with a marriage and many chubby babies."

"We're not together," corrected Falcon, his insides twisting, but the man was already halfway up the hill.

"Yes, my honey-dipped dumpling!" cried the girl, as the man got down on one knee and presented the ring. "Of course I'll spend every day of my life with you."

Faith stood beside Falcon. The scent of peaches lingered. "Isn't love beautiful?"

"Yes," he answered, his gaze glued to Faith as his body warmed. "Love is really something."

A loud echo interrupted his thoughts. He turned just in time to see a dark dome with red cracks cover the entire village.

"It's a chaos dome," squeaked Faith.

"Yes," said Falcon. His body tensed. "Shal-Volcseck is here."

CHAPTER 24

"Lori. Lori. Get up. You hear me? Get up, girl." The blind princess' high-pitched screams were nearing hysteria.

Aya suppressed a tear as she embraced Keira tighter. From across the bridge there was no response from the large silhouette that was Lori.

"I can't see," said Keira.

That's when it hit Aya. Without her bear, Keira was now truly blind.

"I...is she moving? Tell me, A-A-Aya? Is she moving?"

Aya gulped down the rock stuck in her throat. "No."

This only caused Keira to go into an even louder fit of cries and sobs.

Aya remained quiet as she held the princess close. It was about an hour later when a tired Keira finally fell asleep in Aya's arms.

When her eyes finally opened, the sun was barely peeking from over the western mountains.

"We have to go," said Aya.

Keira's cloudy eyes met Aya's. "No. I can't leave her behind. She should at least get a proper burial."

"We can't reach her. We'll come back for her as soon as were done. We're almost at the rendezvous point. We must keep moving so we don't miss it."

"No. She sacrificed herself for me. I won't abandon her."

Aya shook Keira to attention. "She sacrificed herself because she loved you! Do you think this is what she wanted you to do? Sit around feeling sorry for yourself?"

Keira remained quiet as she pursed her lips.

"Don't mock her sacrifice by throwing your life away."

"You're right," said Keira after a minute of silence. "Lori would want me to keep going. She never gave up." She stood. "And neither will I. I will make my uncle pay for killing her."

"Uncle? But it was the natives who killed her," said Aya.

"Those were no natives. Those cannibals were loyal citizens of Sugiko. That was until my uncle had them captured and experimented on."

"Experimented?" asked Aya, clutching her neck.

"Yes. My uncle wishes nothing more than to rule forever. He's been having his scientists test the limits of the human body on many citizens of Sugiko, even children. Many have died, but many others have been turned, their minds twisted beyond repair. Those savages you saw are my uncle's legacy."

"Then we must make haste and put a stop to him."

"But I can't see," said Keira. "Without my sight I won't be able to move as quickly."

"Then I'll be your eyes." Aya threw Keira's arm over her neck, supporting her. "Let's go."

"Lady Hiromy!" called the hair maid. "There you are. We've ransacked the entire castle searching for you."

Hiromy turned toward the elderly lady. By her side stood two other, younger maids. No doubt they were still in training.

"Well," said Hiromy, not bothering to stand from the large stone she lay on. "I've been here all morning." She looked up at the sky, glad she had convinced her father to build her an indoor garden. Directly behind her, the fresh mist floating from the waterfall caressed her skin. Countless native and foreign green plants from across Va'siel provided shade.

"You mustn't sneak about like this, Princess," said the elder lady, signaling for her two pupils to follow. "You know your father wants you to look your best for tonight's ball. And I'm charged with your hair. I will not fail His Highness."

Hiromy caressed her silky hair. "My hair is fine, Nana. You've brushed it twice a day, every day, for the past seventeen years."

"And I would be able to brush it four times a day like I'm supposed to if you didn't insist on spending so much time galloping around with those Rohads." She began brushing her hair as the young maids stood aside, holding pillows filled with dozens of hair pins, combs, and bows. "What would your mother say if she saw you like this?"

"Oh, Nana. You worry too much."

257

"Of course I do." The old lady stopped brushing. "I've known you since you were but a baby. You are like the daughter I've never had."

Hiromy smiled. "You know I love you too, Nana. But I'm not a child. I should be out there on missions, like Falcon and Sheridan."

"Oh, don't speak of that boy here. You know what people say about him."

"You shouldn't believe gossip," said Hiromy. "It's usually not true."

The lady sighed. "I've never understood your obsession with that boy. Even I can see that smitten look in your eyes."

Hiromy plucked a flower from the garden and took a whiff. "I'll have you know that I wasn't thinking of Falcon just now. Someone else has been on my mind."

The elder lady grinned widely. "Oh, yes. Finally. It's that lovely prince from Belwebb, isn't it? That's so much better than a Rohad. I knew you'd come to your senses soon enough, child."

The princess smiled as she tossed the flower into the pond. Images of Sheridan and the dance flashed in her head, causing her skin to goose bump. She still couldn't believe how quickly she had fallen for him.

"Intruder!"

"What was that?" asked one of the hair assistants.

"Intruder. Kill the intr…arrghhh—"

The long, brown doors opened, revealing a creature unlike any Hiromy had ever seen. It had dark-green skin and a vicious face, and it walked on all fours. On her shoulder she carried her wailing father.

"Get the creature," yelled the royal guard captain as he rushed into the room. Half a dozen sword-wielding guards followed.

The muscular kidnapper brought one hand up and swung it, killing the guards and slamming them to the floor.

Two royal wielders joined the fray. The first one shot a burst of water. The second made a mind-wielding symbol Hiromy didn't recognize. The heavy burst of water hit the creature and fell uselessly over the plants.

The kidnapper tossed the emperor aside and rushed her foes. She grabbed them each by the neck. There were two sharp cracks as it snapped their necks like straw. She then turned her attention to the emperor, who cowered in the corner of the room.

"Please," pleaded the emperor. "Whatever you're being paid, I'll triple it."

"This be not about gold," hissed the kidnapper. She moved toward her victim.

Hiromy gritted her teeth. I'll teach you to mess with my dad. She'd lost one parent this way. She wasn't planning on losing another. She stood and dashed toward the creature.

She hopped from rock to rock until she landed in front of the creature.

"No. Not my precious daughter," cried the emperor. "Take me. But leave her out of this. Get out of here, Hiromy!"

"No! Stay behind me, Daddy."

The creature laughed a loud, long cackle. "Yer should listen to that coward, Princess. I be Dokua, leader of the green clansmen, and the most powerful poison wielder yer will ever meet." She gazed behind her. "The entire royal guard be not enough to stop me. A brat who was raised with golden toys will pose no challenge."

Hiromy waved her hand, and in an instant a clear dome of ice covered her father. Another ice block encased her nana and the two assistants.

Dokua growled under her breath. "Foolish, Princess. Once I deliver yer father to the Blood Empress, she be revealing the location of that holy wielder. Nothing is going to stand in my way."

"Wrong. I'm in your way," said Hiromy. She took out both of her bladed fans. "And you're not taking my father."

Dokua banged her chest and rushed forward.

Hiromy stood in place and took aim. Both fans took to the air and slammed into Dokua's forehead. But instead of digging into the bone, the way Hiromy had expected, the weapons bounced off.

Dokua reached Hiromy and took hold of her. She pulled her in, squeezing her into a bear hug. She applied pressure, forcing the life out of Hiromy.

Hiromy closed her eyes. A layer of water forced itself in between the princess and her attacker. The water grew and grew, forcing the poison wielder to widen her grip.

"I will not allow yer to break free," declared Dokua between hisses.

"I wasn't asking for your permission."

The layer of water pushed Dokua back. She let go of her grip as she stumbled back.

Hiromy took a deep breath. The poison wielder's strength was inhuman. She'd been forced to use much more energy than expected.

"Yer be dead!" Dokua crouched and drove at her.

Hiromy water wielded her weapons back into her hand. She threw them directly into her foe's eyes.

"Too predictable," said Dokua, stopping to slap the weapons away.

"Good," answered Hiromy. "I was hoping it was predictable so you wouldn't see what's coming from your right."

"There is nothing on my righttttt…" The creature yelped as a spike of ice drove into her left eye. Misty green liquid burst into the air.

"Unlike your skin, there is no armor in those eyes of yours, huh?"

"Hiromy!" Dokua ground her teeth. "No one has ever bled me. Yer will pay for this." The poison wielder opened her mouth and chanted. An unnaturally long tongue rolled out.

Hiromy brought up her arms to block the unexpected attack, but it proved futile. Dokua's blistered tongue wrapped around Hiromy's neck. Her nose cringed as she took in the aroma of carcasses.

Her vision blurred as the tongue squeezed.

Through shaky hands she willed a layer of water above the poison wielder. The liquid took the form of a long, thin spike as it moved down.

The poison wielder's pupils darted upward in panic. "I'll kill yer before yer can finish yer weak attack." A thick dark gas poured out of Dokua's skin pores.

It flowed into Hiromy's mouth. She felt the tongue's grip loosen ever so slightly. Her chest ached as she forced the spike down with all her might.

There was a loud pained scream. The tongue crashed to the ground, as did Dokua. The ice attack had traveled through the top of her head and out through her torso.

Hiromy stumbled to the floor. The intermingled shouts of her father and nana echoed in her head.

"My little girl!"

"This can't be happening!"

"Someone find the medic!"

The wobbly image of her father came into view. "Don't you worry, baby. Help is on the way."

Then her nana appeared, worry etched in her face. She said some words, but Hiromy understood none. Her heart slowed as her mind grew hazy.

A scream burst in her ears. The image of Sheridan flashed in her mind. A second later, her mind went blank.

CHAPTER 25

"But why would he seal K'vitch?" Falcon asked. Even from the cave he made out the imposing dome.

Shal-Demetrius nodded. "I don't know. There is nothing of value in there that I'm aware of."

"There has to be something," said Faith. "He wouldn't waste time if there wasn't something he craved."

"True," the chaos wielder agreed. "You two need to get in there and find out what happened. Meanwhile I will search for Volcseck out here. Time to finish what I started all those lifetimes ago."

"How can we break into that shield?" Falcon asked.

Demetrius tapped Falcon's emblem. "You're a chaos wielder too, remember? Travel around the dome, looking for the weakest spot on it. Faith will aid you. Now go!"

Falcon and Faith nodded and took off toward the dome. Once they reached it, Falcon steadied himself and concentrated. The grey emblem grew dark with red cracks.

Faith's eyes blinked rapidly as they crept around the dome. "Since we're not sure what we're looking for, keep your eyes open for anything suspicious."

Falcon's hands trembled. "Hey, Faith. Do you think you can do that touch thing you do? I'm having a hard time keeping my composure."

She shrugged. "Sorry. I'm your mentor now, remember? I need to push you a bit."

"What do you mean by that?"

"You heard what Demetrius said. You need to learn to control it yourself during difficult times. At the lake you made some progress, but you must do it when confronted by adversity. I won't always be there."

Falcon sighed. "I suppose you're right."

"Besides, you've done it before. Against your fight with Lao you kept the chaos under control."

The thought of Lao made his chest tighten. "That was different, though. In that fight I took control of water, wind, fire, mind, void, and earth at once. They were all basic elements. I didn't use chaos."

"Don't sell yourself short. You maintained composure. That's an excellent step."

Falcon forced a smile, wishing he had as much confidence in himself as Faith did. As his smile left him, he noticed a red mist emitting from his emblem and flowing to the crack in the dome.

"What is it?" asked Faith, obviously noticing the red trail as well.

"I think I found the opening." He took hold of Faith's hand. "Here, I'll lead us in." He moved forward, easily walking though the wall as if it wasn't there. They came out in a stone-paved road behind a wooden building. Barrels of what appeared to be wine were stacked five rows high. Above, the entire sky was gone as the dome cast a shadowy glare.

"We're in," said Faith, studying her surroundings. "Now what?"

"We go to the town square."

"How about you don't," came a high-pitched snarl.

Falcon turned, recognizing the voice.

Lakirk stood, covering the only way out of the alley. He had an unnaturally long smile that stretched from ear to ear. His right arm was missing, replaced by an octopus-like tentacle. His pupils were yellow with drips of blood. Moist strips of skin hung from his mouth.

Faith gasped.

Lakirk glared at Faith. "Oh, shut it. I'm tired of you, you bucket of rainbows. Life isn't as pure as you make it out to be."

"What on Va'siel did Volcseck do to you?" asked Falcon, covering his nose to suppress the stench flowing from the mayor's son.

Lakirk raised the tentacle to the air. "A gift from Lord Volcseck. I may have been a bit…misguided in believing that Demetrius was the true chaos lord. But now I see the light."

"You're a monster," said Falcon. He couldn't believe some would actually worship Volcseck.

Lakirk's entire body shook as he emitted a strange combination of laughter and sickly coughs. "Funny, that's what

266

Father said right before I..." He licked his blooded lips. "Made him part of me."

Faith clutched her chest. "Your own father...?"

"No. The old imbecile fled after the first bite. But I'll get him. Then I'll get everyone else in this miserable town. It is my reward for being a good servant." His manic eyes stared at Faith. "And I think I'll start with the beautiful one."

Falcon readied for the attack, but it didn't come. Instead, he watched in horror as a tentacle grew where Lakirk's left arm had once been. Blisters bubbled out of his body, shredding his tunic apart. A large eyeball erupted from his chest, darting around without focus.

"Yes!" Lakirk laughed. "This is the power of chaos." Half of his face melted. A thick, yellow liquid oozed out of his skin and dripped on the stone. "Now die!" He pounced.

Falcon called on his water wielding as he froze the floor under the chaos creature, sending it skidding into the barrels. It crashed loudly, sending wood splinters and red wine flying through the air.

A second later, Lakirk emerged from the wreckage. His one remaining eye raged with anger.

Falcon broke the ice apart. He sent every cold block toward the mayor's son.

Lakirk wrapped his tentacles around his body as a shield. The ice bounced of it harmlessly. "My turn." He shot the tentacles forward.

"Fire lance!" At Falcon's command a fire-infused lance appeared above him. It drove forward, pinning one tentacle down. From the corner of his eye he noticed Faith's staff materialize in her hands.

Faith parried the second tentacle. She weaved under it and rushed at Lakirk.

Falcon watched nervously as Faith danced between countless attacks. She's fast!

"Cleanse," said Faith. She brought down the staff on the creature's chest.

Lakirk's body convulsed. His head dropped.

"What did you do?" asked Falcon. He dissolved the fire lance.

"I cleansed the—" Faith's eyes widened. "This can't be." A second later she flew back with tremendous force. Falcon caught her before she hit the ground.

A loud squeal screeched through the alley. "You see?" Lakirk's voice was deep with rage. "Not even holy wielding can handle chaos."

"How are you, Faith?" asked Falcon.

With the staff, she supported herself to her feet. "I underestimated the amount of energy he possessed. Watch out!"

Falcon blocked the tentacle with the broadsword. With his free hand he took out his katana. He sliced upward. The tentacle fell uselessly to the floor.

"How dare you damage me?" Lakirk advanced toward Falcon.

Both warriors locked in a series of blocks, parries, and counterattacks. They continued like that for a minute, neither able to gain the upper hand.

Falcon hopped back. "Lightning dance." The air sizzled as countless moving streaks of lightning moved around the battlefield.

Lakirk screamed as the attacks coursed through his body, lighting his chest with yellow energy. He crashed to the floor.

Falcon took a satisfied breath as he dissolved the lightning.

"You did it!" said Faith.

"Yes, we finally—" The sound of bones snapping in half drenched the air. Falcon wiped his eyes as a giant scorpion pincer burst through Lakirk's back. It was made of palpitating flesh.

The pincer drove down. Oh no! Falcon's skin tingled as he threw himself to the side. The attack switched course and dug deep into his shoulder. Stars burst in his eyes as he dropped to the ground. He tried to move, but his body refused to obey. I'm paralyzed.

The pincer came down toward his chest.

"Celestial Leech!"

A bright light engulfed Falcon's eyes. When he opened them, a large leech had made its way over his chest, shielding him from the attack. He felt the energy from his body slowly return as the white animal tentacles latched on to his arms.

"She will heal you," said Faith. "Stay there for a few minutes."

Faith beat the pincer back with her staff. She created a shield. A second later, it broke apart as the pincer muscled though it.

Faith blocked the attack again. She was breathing heavily. Her hands shook.

Falcon steadied himself as he realized he had to do something or Faith was going to die. She was going one-on-one against the power of Shal-Volcseck. There was no surviving that.

He struggled to his feet.

"No!" cried Faith. "You're not healed yet." An attack came down on her, pushing her against the wall. "If you don't allow the slug take out all the poison, you're going to die."

Another attack forced the staff out of her hands. She wobbled back but remained on her feet.

Falcon gazed at her as he swallowed hard. Regardless of what happened to him, he wouldn't let her die.

"Time for a heat exchange," he mumbled under his breath.

Lakirk looked up, his bloodied eyes wide. "It cannot be. Only Shal-Volcseck possesses those kinds of chaos levels."

The pincer moved toward Falcon.

Before the attack could make contact, Falcon focused on thoughts of Aya and Faith, just as he had practiced. A surge of energy rocked his body. A second later, he felt his body move through thin air at lightning speed. With a puff of smoke, he materialized inside the pincer. Ignoring the rotting stench, he pierced the chunk of meat with his katana. He moved it in a circular motion. The pincer tumbled down, piercing the head of its master.

Lakirk gurgled indistinguishable words. Blood poured out of his mouth. Then his eyes closed.

Falcon teleported out of the pincer. His vision blurred as he stumbled forward. A pair of arms caught him before he fell.

"Falcon. Falcon!" A soft hand ran through his hair as darkness took hold. His body froze. He smiled inwardly, glad Faith's voice was the last voice he would hear.

~~~

His eyes closed, and his body went limp in her arms.

"Falcon!" called Faith. She shook him.

Nothing.

Her voice cracked. "Falcon, wake up!"

Despite her efforts, he remained unmoving.

271

No, no, no. I will not lose you. I will not! With a determination she'd never felt before, she placed her trembling hand on his forehead. She concentrated on thoughts of Falcon as she unleashed her power.

Thoughts of his strong hugs.

Memories of the childhood games they'd played.

Images of them training together.

Suddenly, Falcon's eyes snapped open.

She willed another beat of holy energy through her hands.

Falcon opened his mouth and breathed deeply.

"Don't you ever do that!" she cried. Tears streamed out of her eyes as she held him close. "Ever."

"I won't," mumbled Falcon. "I promise." He remained quiet for a moment. "Faith, you're kind of choking me."

Realizing how hard she was holding him, she released her grip. Her face burned with shame. "Oh, sorry."

"Falcon. Faith!" cried Iris. "You guys did it. You broke the prison wall." Father Lucien ran behind her.

Faith looked up. To her pleasant surprise, the dome was nowhere to be seen.

Father Lucien patted Falcon's back. "I see you figured out my little riddle."

"Err…no, actually, I did not." He coughed loudly. Faith might have healed him, but he still did not feel one hundred percent.

"I think you did. Maybe you did it subconsciously, but you did."

Falcon stared down at Iris, who was now holding both Faith's and Falcon's hands. His eyes widened in recognition. "It's childhood."

Father Lucien nodded. "Yes, it is indeed. Childhood is a phase that seems to last a lifetime, but once we pass it, slips away quickly. We can't get it back, but we can always learn from its innocence and unconditional love. You showed this unconditional love." He looked over at Faith. "I'm sure I know who it was that made you see it."

Falcon shuffled his feet and smoothed down his jacket. His eyes darted from side to side. "So, has anyone seen Demetrius?"

"No," said Iris.

"He's probably back at the cave," said Faith. "We should go tell him what happened."

"Yes."

Both wielders took off in a light jog. Through the town and up the hills they ran. In a few short minutes, they entered the dark cave. Not until they reached the end, did they stop in their tracks.

Faith gasped as she took in her surroundings. The hard wall was broken in a hundred places. All the tubes lay on the floor, broken and useless. "What happened here?"

A pained grunt reached her ears. She dragged her feet toward the noise, fearful that she already knew what it was.

"You!" cried Falcon.

Faith cringed back at the horrible sight. Demetrius lay on the floor, a sword sticking out of his stomach. Volcseck stood over him.

"Yes, me," said the overly calm voice. Volcseck faced them. A grin was the only thing that could be seen under the hood of his dark robe. "I must thank you both."

Faith forced her mouth open. "Thank us?"

"Yes. I needed a chaos element. I couldn't use mine, of course. That would have killed me. But now I have one." He caressed the dirt-stained chaos element he held in his hands. Thank you for leading me to it."

"You will never get away with this," mumbled Demetrius.

Volcseck looked down at his former master. "Oh, I think I will. You should have stopped me when you had the chance. Now it's too late."

"What would your mother say?"

Faith staggered as Volcseck's grin turned stern. There was a long silence. "She is of no matter. Now all I need is one element." He pointed at Faith. "Holy."

Falcon stood in front of Faith, sword drawn.

Volcseck's smirk returned. "Don't you worry, Falcon Hyatt, is it? I'm not taking her yet. But soon, very soon." With those last words, he disappeared in a mist of dark smoke.

Faith dashed toward Demetrius. Maybe there was still time to save him.

"No," said Demetrius weakly. "Let me go. I'm tired of living. It's time I join my love." He looked over at Falcon. "It's up to you to keep her safe, youngling. Do you understand?"

"Yes, sir."

Demetrius took Faith's hands. "Keep an eye on him. You must guide him. He'll be lost without you."

Faith nodded, unable to form words.

"Watch out for one another." His lips ceased moving as his eyes slowly closed.

Faith's chest ached as she looked down at the lifeless master they'd barely known. She didn't say a word. She just held Falcon's trembling hand, wishing she could do something to make him forget about his pain.

CHAPTER 26

"My vision is coming back," declared Keira, her voice hopeful. "That means we're getting close to Aykori and Draiven. I see everyone. They set up camp and are waiting for us."

Aya's insides burst with joy. She had been helping Keira move for the past few hours, and her legs were ready to give out on her. "What way?"

"Go left."

The girls walked a few more minutes before they heard voices. They shoved a few palms aside and came out in a large camp. About a hundred men sat in huddled circles by tents.

"Keira!" shouted Rika. In seconds she had her small arms wrapped around Keira's thin frame. "I knew ya were going to make it. I just knew it. Nothing could keep her down, I said to them. Nothing."

"Thank the creator," cried Nanake, as she too embraced her granddaughter in a hug. She then took a step back. "Are you well? You two look like you been through a fire gauntlet."

Keira remained quiet as her gaze turned to the ground. "I think is better we don't speak of that at the moment. The important thing now is that we're back."

"Wait," said Nanake. Her eyes darted about. "Where is Lori?"

The girl's silence was the only answer that was needed. Rika fell to the floor, sobbing loudly.

A set of tears escaped Nanake. She wiped them away. "Perhaps we should call this entire attack off."

"No!" cried Keira. "Lori and many of our fallen brothers and sisters died for this. I won't let it be in vain."

Dozens of soldiers nodded in approval. Behind the crowd towered Raji, looking as stern as ever.

The crowd parted as the two bears made their way forward.

Keira walked forward and met them. She caressed the brown bear. "I'm sorry, Aykori." With her other hand she patted the black bear's tangled fur. "I'm sorry to you too, Draiven. I let your sister die. I understand if you hate me."

The princess seemed to disappear in the bears' massive bodies as they enveloped her in a hug. Once the bears moved back, Keira once again appeared. Both her animals stood by her side, the massive Aykori on her left, and the even larger Draiven on her right.

"My uncle has brought suffering to a time of peace!" The men listened attentively. "No more! Tonight we will march on him and stop this injustice. No more of our people will be experimented on. No more of our people will be put to the torch for speaking against tyranny. No more of our people will be crucified for not bowing to Hotaru. No more of our children will starve as my uncle and his men eat in abundance." Keira held her hand to the air. "No more!"

The thunderous shouts of soldiers fused with the vicious growls of bears, creating a cheer against tyranny unlike any Aya had ever heard before.

~~~

The girls met at the middle of the camp under the twinkling stars. Both had bathed in the river and snuck in a few hours of sleep.

"Are you ready?" Keira asked.

Aya nodded. "Of course."

"Good."

Rika, Raji, Aykori, and Draiven joined the girls.

"The time is here, men!" cried Keira. "We do not have the numbers to win in an open battle. But it will be up to you to hold them off and take their attention as we sneak behind their lines and take out Hotaru. Many of you will not live to see the morning sun. I'm sorry for that."

"We know the risks, Princess!" yelled a man from the crowd. "It will be an honor to die if we must."

Keira pumped her fists. "Let's go get our home back."

Aya went over to Sheridan. "How are you feeling?"

Sheridan forced a smile. "A little nervous. Leading an army isn't really my forte. Hyatt is more suited for that kind of thing."

Aya patted him on his arm, which seemed to relax him a bit. "You'll do fine."

"Hey!" called Keira. "Let's go. We don't have another minute to waste."

Aya waved goodbye and joined the small infiltration group.

"Good fortunes to you," called Nanake as they took off on their trek.

They walked through the misty forest in silence for over an hour. Aya was surprised at the quietness of the large bears' footsteps. She supposed it must have been part of their training. Even Raji's steps were muted.

"Here's the cave," said Keira.

Aya scanned the rocks, looking for it.

"It's right here," said Rika, rolling her eyes. She walked around a corner and disappeared. "Sometimes I wonder who the blind one is."

"It's an illusion," Keira clarified. "From an angle it appears that there is nothing there."

Aya followed the bears and blind girl into the musky cave. Her hands raced to her nose as the fetid stench reached her.

"This cave leads to the castle sewers," said Keira, noticing Aya's discomfort. "From there we can use the hidden trapdoor to infiltrate the castle."

279

They moved at a steady pace for most of the day. Aya made it a point to breathe through her nose. It seemed that the deeper they went into the cave, the stronger the smell became. She was so engrossed with the stench that she barely registered the lack of soft thuds behind her. She turned to find Raji removing his two massive axes from the back where they hung.

"What are you doing?" said Aya.

Everyone else stalled and looked back.

"We have been followed for some time now," Raji growled.

"Damn," said Keira. "They knew we were coming and waited until we were trapped inside to make their move."

"We're not the ones who are trapped," thundered Raji. Dozens of armored soldiers materialized out of the shadows. Aya made out all kinds of weapons in their hands: spears, broadswords, sais, nets, halberds, and many other killing tools she'd never seen before.

"Go," ordered Raji. "No one will follow you."

Keira stepped forward. "But…"

Raji looked back at her with without saying a word. Aya knew that a silent understanding had passed between them.

"Let's move, everyone." This time she did not look back.

"But there must be over one hundred soldiers back there," said Rika, her complexion pale.

"She's right," added Aya. "Is it really a good idea to leave him alone?"

"Raji knows what he's doing," said Keira. "I believe in him; you should too."

Aya gulped, hoping that Raji would be fine. If the soldiers got through him, it would force Keira to abandon her mission in order to fight to stay alive.

The group once again pressed forward. Moments later the sounds of weapons clattering and shouts echoed through the walls. Aya thought she heard Raji's loud grunts from time to time, but she wasn't sure. As they continued to move, the sounds died off, replaced by a chilling silence.

"I see it," whispered Rika. She dusted off a layer of dirt and grime on the floor, revealing a large, square metal door. There was no lock or handle on it. "Now what?"

"Rika, you do your thing," Keira ordered. She pointed at a dark hole in the corner of the cave. If it hadn't been for Keira, Aya doubted she would have seen it. "Why do you think I insisted you come with me? I need that small frame of yours."

Rika smirked. "I won't let ya down." She crawled on all fours and forced her body inside the hole.

"Wow," said Aya. "I didn't think she was going to fit in there."

Keira grinned. "Yes. She can squeeze through anything."

There was a loud clatter from inside the metal door. Seconds later the door squeaked up an inch.

"Help me," whimpered Rika. "This thing is heavyyyyy!"

Aya and Keira took hold of the door and pulled. Sweat formed on their foreheads as they strained to no avail.

Suddenly a black paw took hold of the door. It became as light as air as it flung open and clattered on the other side of the floor, raising a plume of dust.

"Great job, Draiven," thanked Keira as she hopped into the hole. "You too, Rika."

Aya followed the princess into the hole, followed by Draiven and Aykori. Once on the other side, she scanned her surroundings. They appeared to be in a library. The walls were stacked with countless books. Dozens of oak tables were spread out throughout the large room.

"This is where we part ways, Rika. We have to go after 'em on our own now."

"But…but I need to go with ya."

Keira bent down and caressed her cousin's cheeks. "No. You did your part, now I have to do mine. Stay here where it's safe." Rika pouted at first, but a moment later she gave Keira a hug and took a seat on the patterned floor.

Keira stood before the brown bear. "You stay here with her, Aykori. I need you to protect her." The bear growled softly, but did as he was asked. "See you two in a bit."

Aya bit her lower lip, hoping that Keira's words would come true and she would return to her loved ones, though she was sure that there was a high probability they wouldn't. If only she had her wielding.

They snuck out of the library and hurried through large, golden double doors and through a luxurious hall filled with jade statues. Minutes later, they reached a set of long stairs.

They ran up the red carpet, twisting up the circular stairs for what seemed an eternity.

"Finally!" cried Keira as they reached the last step. They stood in a long corridor adorned with dozens of paintings. Silk yellow curtains hung in front of the many windows.

"Where is it?"

"Past those doors," said Keira, pointing at two giant doors that stood open at the end of the hallway. "Let's go, Draiven."

The bear snarled, exposing his sharp fangs. He took off, followed closely by both girls.

Aya slowed her pace as she entered the throne room. It was large, nearly empty, and had a magnificent red-and-white tile floor. Tapestries depicting dragons and tigers adorned the walls. The left side of the room had a large opening with an oval balcony.

From the opening Aya saw Keira's soldiers engaged in battle against Hotaru's forces. Beside them there was a large ocean, extending as far the eye could see.

"Hello, niece," came a loud sneer. "I see you made it past my little trap in the caves."

Aya forced herself to look away from the ensuing battle and toward the voice. At the end of the room sat an overly fat man atop a grand throne. He was short and completely bald. A long mustache dangled at both sides of his lips.

At the sight of him, Draiven took off on all fours. But a few short feet away from reaching him, a cage sprang from under the floor. The bear slammed viciously into the thick bars that now encased him. Draiven shrugged and stood, pushing on the bars.

"I see you're still using those savage beasts," said Hotaru. "All muscle and no brain."

Keira's balled fists turned white. "The only savage I see here is you." Her voice dripped with anger. "How could you betray your own family?"

Hotaru yawned. "No vision, just like your useless father?" He brought out a short scroll and tossed it. It rolled to Keira's feet.

"What is this?" she asked.

"That, my dear niece, is a binding contract. By signing it you relinquish the city to me. I hold power here in Sugiko, but the Va'siel consul won't recognize me as the leader unless I have a signed contract."

Keira kicked the scroll aside. "I will never hand over my father's kingdom."

"I thought you might say that." Hotaru grabbed a handful of blueberries from his bowl and stuffed them in his mouth. Purple juice squirted down his lips as he pointed to the battle raging outside. "You see your men? They're all going to die. Their blood as well as your grandmother's will be on your hands."

Keira gulped.

"I can save them." He smiled, revealing a series of yellow teeth. "All you have to do is sign the contract."

Despite her initial apprehension, Keira looked up, her fiery gaze meeting her uncle's. "How about I just kill you?"

Hotaru grimaced. "Have it your way, then. Senjubo. Baka!"

At his command two men emerged from behind the throne. One wore a brown mask that obscured his eyes and nose. The other had a squared jaw and deep scars on his face. But what shocked Aya wasn't their faces; it was their blue uniforms.

"You're Rohads?" asked Aya, unable to suppress the unexpected surge of anger brewing inside her.

The one with the brown mask brought up his hands. "Yes, I'm Senjubo of the Missea Rohads."

Aya gritted her teeth. "How dare you use the title of Rohad. You're a disgrace to everything we stand for."

Senjubo turned to his companion. "It appears that Rohads over at our sister academy in Ladria are not too bright." He cackled loudly.

Hotaru stood. His flabby chin dangled uselessly as he opened his mouth. "Senjubo and Baka understand that money and power are the meaning of life." He pointed at Aya. "You're a Rohad too. Abandon this losing fight and join me. You hold no allegiance to my niece. I can make you wealthier than a lifetimes of missions will ever make you."

Aya's eyes blazed. "My loyalty is to my friends, not to gold."

"Have it your way. Kill them."

Senjubo rushed at Aya. Baka took after Keira.

A block of earth appeared under Senjubo, tossing him through the air. Once in the air, he flapped his arms. Blocks of rock appeared behind him. They shot forward.

So he's an earth wielder. Aya dashed out of the way at the last second. To her right, Keira had just dodged a mind wave.

Hotaru gargled loudly. He caressed a stone in his hands. "This little special emblem allows all my men to wield. You have no chance."

A glove of hard rock encased Senjubo's hands. He swung in precise attacks. "Give it up. I owned all the martial arts records during my time at the academy."

Aya dodged a knee. She weaved around two punches. Seeing an opening on his left side, she moved in. A hard punch sent her tumbling back.

Senjubo chuckled. "Falling for the classic feints. You new Rohads are truly pathetic."

A wave of sand wrapped Aya's arms and legs.

Senjubo waved his sand toward him as he took out a long knife that hung under his waist. He brought Aya face to face with him. "And now you have no weapons."

Aya rocked her neck back. She brought it forward as fast as she could. There was a loud crunch as both the Rohads' foreheads met. The sand dissolved.

Her kick landed on Senjubo's jaw. He threw a wild punch. Aya grabbed his arm. She wrapped her hand around it and flipped him onto the floor. Before he could react, she pounced. The crunching sound of bones filled the air as Aya broke both of Senjubo's wrists. Still on the floor, she flipped over to his legs. Her hands locked around his knees as she applied pressure. The sounds came again.

"Aaaaarghhh…You broke my—"

An elbow to the face rendered her adversary unconscious. "You talk too much." Aya stood. "And by the way, I broke all those records."

287

Hotaru held up his hands. "Hey, wait a minute. Let's be reasonable about this."

Aya took after him.

Click!

By the time she realized what was going on, the bars had already encased her.

"Got you!" cheered Hotaru. His belly jiggled as he laughed.

From inside the cage Aya breathed a sigh of relief as she noticed Keira standing over Baka. She might have been trapped, but at least Keira was free to finish off her uncle.

"Ooops!" said a high-pitched voice. Aya turned just as Hotaru threw a thick tapestry over the cage with the bear, covering it entirely. "I'm sorry, niece. Did you need your monster to see?"

A loud crack echoed as Baka kicked Keira on the face. She staggered back.

"Let's so how you like this. Waves of the mind!" Clear ripples flew from Baka and slammed into Keira's chest.

Keira staggered back.

"Tough girl, I see," said Baka. "I've never seen anyone survive that. But you won't survive this next attack. Bloody nightmare!"

Aya gasped as purple tentacles stretched from Baka's head. She had learned of this particular attack from books. It was widely used on criminals as a slow, painful form of torture.

Keira shrieked as the first tentacle pierced her torso. Blood splattered to the floor. The tentacle retracted and another moved in. The second one pierced her hand and moved back. Another gush of blood dripped to the pristine tile.

"To your left, no, to your right!" cried Aya. But her instructions were having no effect. The blind princess stood in a defensive position. But the attacks were too fast and unpredictable.

"Ahhhhhhhhhhhh!"

Aya cringed at the pained scream. She had never seen anyone take so much punishment.

"How are you still standing?" yelled Baka. Two tentacles dug under her elbows.

Keira wobbled from side to side. Blood oozed from a half a dozen holes in her body. "I'm not going to let my people down. My friends...my family..."

"Will be dead!" finished the false emperor. "Finish it, Baka."

"As you wish."

The bear growled and the cage shook uncontrollably.

"Don't give up, Keira," cried Aya. "You can win."

"I...I can't see..."

"So what? The girl I fought wouldn't have given up just because she couldn't see. The Keira I know wouldn't let something like that stand in the way of freeing her city."

289

"How touching," said Baka, "but it's over." He pushed all eight tentacles forward.

To Aya's surprise, Keira didn't appear scared anymore. Her feet were steady. Her hands rested on her side. A grin spread across her lips.

The tentacles moved as one. Keira rolled under the attack. The tentacles followed, each moving in for the kill.

Aya's heart raced as Keira expertly weaved between attacks, while closing in on her opponent.

Baka's legs trembled.

Hotaru stood from his throne. "Get her, imbecile. She's a blind girl!"

Keira front-flipped over a purple mass and landed in front of the mind wielder. The tentacles rushed in. Keira grabbed Baka and threw him over her. He yelped as his own tentacles entered his chest. He crashed to the floor. A pool of blood spread from his corpse.

Keira turned her gaze to Hotaru.

"This is not over." Hotaru picked up a crossbow that rested at his feet. "I will not lose my empire." He pointed the crossbow at his niece. "Any last words?"

Aya closed her eyes. If Keira could do it, then so could she.

She calmed her mind as she clasped her hands. She searched within her, focusing her energy. At first all she saw was pitch black. She refined her thoughts. Energy. Then she saw it. It was nothing but a blue speck floating in a sea of darkness. She willed her thoughts into it, and slowly it grew. A bright light coursed inside her chest and her body tingled with the familiar feeling.

"What is that noise?" Hotaru gazed at the battlefield. He ran toward the balcony, his eyes glued on the massive tsunami that had risen from the sea. "But that's impossible. It would take an entire army of gifted water wielders to do something like that. Who? Who?" His gaze turned to Aya. "You!"

Aya's hands trembled with exhaustion as she divided the water into hundred of ice spears. She guided all of them toward the enemy soldiers.

An ice attack entered the room and slammed into the throne chair, shattering it into hundreds of pieces. A soon as it broke, the steel bars snapped open. As Aya had suspected, the chair had the controls to the cages.

Hotaru whimpered as he crawled to the edge of the balcony. "You must tell me how you broke through the devourer's blockade." His eyes darted over to Keira and Draiven, who were closing in on him. "N...n...niece. Surely you un...understand that what I did was...was...was for the g...good of Sugiko."

Keira remained expressionless. "Get out of here. Never come back to my father's lands."

"Of course." His eyes faced the floor as he crawled away. "But I'm taking you with me!"

Hotaru stood, driving toward Keira with a dagger in hand.

Draiven dashed forward and took Hotaru in his paws. He held him up for a second, and then he tossed the screaming man toward the rocky cliffs.

Aya winced as the screams came to a bone-crushing end.

Keira stumbled to the edge of the balcony. She looked out at the battlefield. "The city is ours!"

Her men from the beach cheered. Hotaru's soldiers held their hands up in defeat, as they eyed the sharp ice spear above them.

A load of weight left Aya's shoulders, and for the first time in days, she allowed herself to smile.

CHAPTER 27

Night had enveloped the sky as Keira walked up the steps. It was weird for Aya to see her in a fine silk dress. Even stranger was seeing her wear makeup around her almond eyes. It wasn't much, but Aya still found it hard to get used to.

The large crowd that had gathered in the bazaar stood quiet, watching as the rightful ruler took her place.

Keira reached the top steps. Nanake, Raji, Rika, and her two bears were already there, waiting for her. She turned to face her people.

Nanake stepped to the front of the podium and spoke in a much louder voice than Aya expected from an elder. "All hail Empress Keira, the eighty-seventh of her line. May her rule be a long and prosperous one!"

The crowd erupted in thunderous applause.

Keira stepped forward and waited for the applause to dwindle. "It is an honor to serve you. I promise to do my best to continue my father's legacy, a legacy of justice, toleration, and kindness. This victory would not have been possible without the hundreds of men and women who fought against tyranny." She smiled as she gazed at Raji, Rika, and her bears. Her voice grew shaky. "Many others had to give their lives."

Many from the crowd looked down in sadness. No doubt they too had lost loved ones.

Nanake waved her hand. At her call a woman emerged from the crowd. In her hands she carried a cuddly bear cub. The bear had snowy-white fur, just like Lori once had. The woman presented the cub to Keira.

"It's Lori's daughter," said Nanake. "Her name is Maru."

Aya felt a warm feeling creep all over her as Keira took the cub in her arms. She held it close, as if afraid to lose it. She whispered something in her ear, though Aya was too far to hear what it was.

"Thank you, Grandma," said Keira. "But there is someone else I should thank for this victory. Rohads, come forward."

Sheridan and Aya stepped up to the podium.

"These Rohads showed courage unlike any I've ever seen before. It's no exaggeration to say that without 'em, Hotaru would still be terrorizing Sugiko." She took out two jade pins. The insignia of a dragon was imprinted on them. She carefully pinned them on the Rohads' chests. "I declare Aya and Sheridan honorary members of the Sugiko army." She then faced her crowd. "Enough formalities. As my first order I declare that the warehouses shall be re-opened. Each head of their household will be given enough rice to feed their families for a year. Let the celebrations begin!"

The people cheered louder than ever. Aya could have sworn that she saw Raji almost smile for a split second as the people took to the street in dance. Others watched as multicolored fireworks burst in the air. A large red dragon with men underneath it weaved through the street, followed behind by countless laughing children.

Aya marched over to Keira. A sense of sadness washed over her. "This is where I say my goodbye."

"Are you sure you can't stay a while longer?"

"You have your empire to look after. And I have people I need to get back to." The thought of seeing Falcon made her heart skip a beat.

"Of course, you have your responsibilities." Keira's expression grew stern. "I hope that what you told me about the Suteckh Empire doesn't come to pass. But if they attack, then you'll have the full support of my army."

"Thank you," said Aya, glad to have Sugiko's support.

"No. Thank you for showing me kindness when I showed you nothing but spite." Keira embraced Aya. "You will always have a sister in me."

Behind them, Rika shuffled her shaky feet. Aya extended her hand and pulled her into the hug. "We can all be sisters."

"But I was horrible to ya," stuttered Rika.

Aya smiled. "I've already forgotten about all that. How about we make new memories from now on?"

"I like that."

"Can I join in on that hug?" asked Sheridan, laughing to himself.

The girls eyed him without saying a word.

"Yeah, didn't think so, but I had to give it a shot." He walked into the crowd, dancing and singing at the top of his lungs.

~~~

"I'm going to miss this place," said Aya. From atop the mountain they had a clear view of the castle, though it looked much smaller from so far away. The fireworks were still bursting every few seconds.

Sheridan stuffed a peach dumpling into his mouth. "It was nice and all, but I need to get back to my love."

"Your love?" Aya asked. She sneezed as dry pollen blew into her nose. It smelled of honey.

"Hiromy, of course. Oh, how I missed that hair, those eyes, and that tight suit that hugs her fine body and—"

Aya brought up her hand. "I think I get the idea."

"Oh, yes. Sorry."

"Let's keep moving. We're still days away from Ladria."

"You mean we're not going to stop at the Butha bathing houses?" He kicked the ground under him. "Sheesh. You really have to learn to relax. We accomplished our mission and gained the support of Sugiko for the upcoming battle. I'm sure the Ghost Knight also secured the aid of Yangshao. What else do you want?"

"There is no time for bath houses. We might have won the battle, but the war is far from over. The Suteckh and Shal-Volcseck are far from done. Of that I'm certain."

~~~

"May you rest in peace," said Father Lucien. He lit sticks of lavender incense over the stacks of rocks. Underneath rested a wooden coffin.

It had been a week since the chaos master had passed away. Falcon took in the strong smell of flowers. Usually he would have waved it away, but today it didn't bother him as much. Even though he had not known Demetrius for a long time, the old man had taught him an important lesson. Being a chaos wielder didn't necessarily mean he had to be evil. Before him lay a being that had been a chaos wielder, yet he'd been a good man. This gave him hope for the future. Hope that he did not have to give in to the power of chaos. Hope that with holy guiding him, the chaos within him could be kept under control.

"Let's go," he said, walking out of the cave. He moved through the long corridor in silence. Faith, Iris, and Father Lucien did the same.

When they walked out of the cave, it had already begun to rain. Small pieces of hail bounced off his head. He held up his hands as the ice balls fell on his palm. Aya suddenly filled his thoughts. What was she doing now? He longed to see her again. To show her what he'd learned. It had been so long since they had last spoken.

"Hey, mate!"

Falcon looked up in surprise. Off in the distance, running toward him from K'vitch, was a small figure.

"Mates!"

"Chonsey," said Falcon, waving at his friend. He certainly was happy to see him, but shocked. Chonsey should still be back at the academy, training for the next trials.

Chonsey stopped in front of him, gasping for breath. "I finally found you, mate."

"What are you doing here?"

"That's why I'm here." The cloth of his shirt wrinkled as he tightened his grip on it.

Falcon didn't like the tone of his friend's voice. "Out with it!"

"The Suteckh launched an attack on Ladria, mate."

Falcon's stature slumped. "What?"

"They destroyed everything. They even tried to kidnap the emperor, but Hiromy put a stop to it."

His chest tightened. "Is she alive?"

"I...I don't know. But what I do know is that the entire city has been annihilated, and thousands of lives have been lost."

Falcon looked at the sky absently as Chonsey's words echoed in his head.

"Ladria has been sacked."

THE WIELDING ADVENTURE CONTINUES!!!!!

Don't miss the epic conclusion to the Void Wielder Trilogy!

-Book 3, Heir of the Elements is available now on Amazon!

~About The Author~

Cesar Gonzalez lives in Bakersfield, California, with his space-wielding son. To learn more about Cesar and see artwork from Element Wielder, visit his website at **http://cesarbak99.wix.com/element-wielder**

Become a full-fledged Rohad by joining Cesar Gonzalez' e-mail newsletter (visit website or follow link). **Members will receive 2 free books.**

http://wix.us9.list-manage2.com/subscribe?u=f4ec4abf3f25dccaad395c259&id=a3134c0c4b

1. **Book 1- Dawn of the Lost (Prequel to THE LOST AND THE WICKED).**

2. **Book 2- The Lightning General.** (A short story following Falcon's master: K'ran Ryker.) Will be released to members of the newsletter soon).

Other Books By Cesar Gonzalez

Void Wielder Trilogy:

-Legacy of the Golden Wielder: Prequel to the Void Wielder Trilogy.

-Legacy of Chaos (Book 2 of the Void Wielder Trilogy)

-Heir of The Elements: Book 3 Of the Void Wielder Trilogy.

STAR RISING SERIES-

Star Rising: Heartless (Available for pre-order now)

THE LOST AND THE WICKED SERIES:

The Lost And The Wicked- (Available now!)

Year: 2107

When 16-year-old Mandy Glau returns to Earth after a six-year space expedition, she can't wait to get back to her normal teenage life. But she never could have foreseen what would transpire.

Mandy's ship, holding her sisters and two hundred crew members, sinks into the bottom of the Pacific. Mandy escapes, only to find that the Earth she knew is no more. It has been destroyed and is now devoid of human life. Once proud cities now lie tattered in ruins, shells of their former selves. And a new diabolical species has taken residence in her former home planet.

Mandy must now race against the clock as she struggles to get her family and crew free from the sunken ship, the same ship that only has two weeks left of air supply. But now a new evil is hunting her, determined to end humanity once and for all.

47364061R00184

Made in the USA
Middletown, DE
28 August 2017